Interruptions in Life

INTERRUPTIONS IN LIFE

Copyright © 2017 Bernard Dennis Boylan

First Edition, April, 2018

All rights reserved, including the right to reproduce this book, or portions thereof, in any form.

Interruptions in Life

A Trilogy

Bernard D. Boylan

Table of Contents………………...*Interruptions in Life*

Story I: **Dauntless:** a Naval Cadet and Two Sisters

Story II: **Shad Point:** The Belated Advent of Love

Story III: **Kokoncke:** Dodkins' Lost Sheep

INTERRUPTIONS IN LIFE

INTERRUPTIONS IN LIFE

Dauntless:
A Naval Cadet And Two Sisters

A Novella

Bernard D. Boylan

2008, 2015, 2017

INTERRUPTIONS IN LIFE

Preface:

This is the story of how a family "conglomerate" began. Jack Connerty, a financial executive who kept his family loose with corny jokes, while sorting out conversational nuances; Mary, his wife who trained her girls to be modern; the daughters, Darby and Jeanne, who developed different personalities and views and competed for Derek Hanson, an English naval cadet. All saw the thread-thin line between "life and void."

I wish to thank the librarians at Morton Public (the best in the area) for their daily help; the supervisor at Houghton Cemetery for patiently giving directions three times to Tom Sherrill's grave; and myself for having fun while creating American fiction, instead of being subjected to criticism for historical incorrectness, the lack of documentation, and footnotes.

INTERRUPTIONS IN LIFE

INTERRUPTIONS IN LIFE

Table of Contents.............................*Dauntless*

1. Touchdown—Houghton, Connecticut
2. Epsom Derby—A Sip of the Salts
3. Darby Connerty & Derek Hanson
4. St. Bridget's and Houghton Square
5. Jeanne Connerty / Soup Kitchen
6. Dartmouth, Devon, England
7. Houghton Village
8. Walking on Warren Street
9. Noon at the Historical Society; the Moors
10. Derek's Family
11. Tom Sherrill
12. HMS Dauntless
13. Darby's Despair
14. An Injury
15. Mary Connerty
16. Jeanne D' Arc
17. The Economy
18. Morton Point
19. Decision Time for Derek
20. Epilogue—Four Years Later

    Sources

INTERRUPTIONS IN LIFE

Chapter 1: Touchdown, Houghton, Connecticut

When Derek Hanson, a British Naval Cadet, asked, "Is anything going on tonight?" The attendant at the Navy Lodge answered, "There's a mixer tonight at Plant College across the Thames River. They say that girls can get planted! A bus leaves in an hour for the dance."

It was late June and Derek was beginning a tour of U.S. Naval installations on the East Cost, including the Subase and the Coast Guard. Although tired from traveling, never bashful and always personable, Derek went to the dance.

Stationing herself at the door, a tall thin flashy blonde, Darby, spotted him and asked for the first dance. He was taller, thin, 21, athletic, with black hair, and a square jaw. He looked the part of a naval officer. Darby discovered a veritable trophy and like a spoiled child, wanted him. She monopolized dances with him and afterward, took Derek aside, "Would you like to sample American hospitality at my family's mansion in Houghton village?"

"Whoa!" Derek said cautiously. "Let's move slower. Pick me up at 8:30 a.m. at the Navy lodge. Then I'll determine if you're as beautiful in sunlight as you are tonight." His compliment danced in her mind until sleep.

On the next day, when Darby and her sister Jeanne brought Derek home, the jock next door called. "Can your Naval boyfriend complete the roster for the last touch football game of the season? We're desperate because two guys are traveling. It's at the Morton Walking Track."

"I've never played but sure! I'll try." Derek was glad to exercise. Beforehand, he wondered what mongrel of rugby or English football the Yanks had devised.

The chilly June, 2008 afternoon was an anomaly. It wasn't an almanac entry of the past Winter or prediction of the Summer to come. The northerly breeze gusted at the Morton walking track. For the past two weeks, the skies had been unusually blue and the temperatures moderate.

"I don't think Spring is over," said Darby.

Derek asked, "Does it get much colder?"

"Colder than an English tit," teased Darby. However, the warm spell returned the next day. The track was a half-mile rectangle, boxing in lacrosse, soccer, and junior league football fields on its infield.

Darby wore a gray parka with an Alice-blue inner hood that showed off her blonde hair. Her younger sister Jeanne, who had her long black hair twisted in a French braid, wore a plain, green, three-quarter length walking coat. They stopped frequently to watch the young men relive their boyhoods while playing touch football.

"What's Derek doing in the States?" Jeanne asked.

"He's on a naval tour."

The touch football players, wearing faded gray athletic parkas, good naturedly yipped over scores or near misses. Watching their boyish antics was pure entertainment for the girls. One of the passes was tipped upwards and caught, resulting in a touchdown. "Good going, Limey!" roared his teammates. Derek, the naval cadet from the Royal Naval Academy in Dartmouth, Devon, (Southwest England), made the play, even though it was his first touch football game.

"How did you like touch football?' the girls asked.

"I'm promoting cross-Atlantic athletic fellowship," grinned Derek. "I'm pleasantly surprised at its fun, exercise, and simple rules."

Derek asked, "Where do you girls go to school?"

"At first," Darby said, "We received private schooling: eight grades at Hazel Point; Then four at Houghton High School. Before my senior year, I read Dad's financial magazines and sized up the business scene. Most of the money flow is going to Southeast Asia. I decided Mandarin was the language of the future and chose Plant College for its Chinese major. In the fall I'll be a sophomore. During the summer, I'm taking advanced classes.

Derek also questioned quiet Jeanne, Darby's sister. "I attended the same schools and get good grades, but I'm stumped about a career and college. I volunteer at the soup kitchen in the city on Sunday evenings.

INTERRUPTIONS IN LIFE

It was no accident that tall Darby was attracted to Derek Hanson and brought him home after the Saturday mixer. She was fascinated by uniforms and boys taller than her. She told her Mom: "My new friend Derek is two inches taller, has terrific poise, manners, and a willingness to learn, to try new things."

Mary warned, "If he's that good, don't scare him away with your antics."

INTERRUPTIONS IN LIFE

Chapter 2: Epsom Derby—a Sip of the Salts. England, 1990

Located 13.6 miles southwest of Charring Cross, London, the Epsom Derby Racecourse is a turf track in Epsom Downs, Surrey, for 3-year-old thoroughbreds, racing clockwise, contrary to the American style. Racing has been held there since 1780. It was named after the Earl of Derby and is usually called the Derby, the richest most prestigious race in England, part of the English triple crown. "Downs" is the name of the range of hills and town. A spring of mineral water containing magnesium sulfate was boiled to extract the mineral, used for baths, beauty, soreness, and removing splinters. When the Queen makes a royal visit, a highlight of the London social season, a dress code is observed. "What was that dress code?" Jack asked.

Their young dinner guest replied, "The code for the Queen's Stand Investec Derby Day is either black or grey morning dress with a top hat— it's traditional and obligatory for gentlemen on Derby Day. Ladies are asked to wear a formal day dress, or a trouser suit, with a hat or substantial fascinator. The management asks that guests be informed, beforehand."

Jack Connerty was a financial broker trying hard to become a director. Between races, he was finalizing details of an office lease in the new financial district in London. Although infused with the bloom of motherhood, pregnant Mary had accompanied Jack for months, but was getting more nervous as the day dragged on. "Jack, Let's go! I'm beginning to get cramps!"

But he thought it was a false alarm and insisted, "In a minute! We've almost finalized the deal."

Their daughter Darby's name is unique—she was named for the Epsom Derby. She was born prematurely in the paddock area while her loquacious father Jack was negotiating. Jack succeeded in setting up the branch, but Mary never let him forget it. For years, Darby's father joked with guests, "I should have taken a chance on the Irish Sweepstakes instead of letting Mary bathe in the Epsom salts. One bath and a baby girl bounced out. She's been a bouncing baby girl ever since!"

Mary quickly spoke up: "Find another joke, Jack; that one is wearing thin. And I only took a sip of the water."

"Then, you must have imbibed," laughed Jack.

(Note: the Irish Sweepstakes were established in 1930 to benefit hospital care. But in 1966, an expose published in "Fortune" magazine revealed that only 5 to 10 percent of the proceeds went to charity; the private company skimmed the rest. The slow motion scandal resulted in voluntary liquidation in 1987.)

INTERRUPTIONS IN LIFE

Chapter 3: Darby Connerty & Derek Hanson

During parties in the village, liquor flows freely. Two years ago, a drunken friend date-raped Darby, but she didn't press charges because of the notoriety. Since then, she's had sex with others.

When Derek arrived, she kissed him so often that he memorized her features: blonde hair falling over green eyes, a delicate chin, high cheek bones, a flawless complexion, a pretty nose, and dimples.

Like many first-borns, Darby was indulged and spoiled; she knew what she wanted and nagged until she got it. On Sunday morning, her blonde hair was tied in ponytails. Darby had a classic face and a thin frame, but was too restless and flippant to be a model.

Darby hated delinquent teens, who yelled "titless wonder!" She yelled back "dickless homo!"

With her long legs, Darby outraced all the other girls at field hockey. She loved competition, but of course, field hockey isn't a commercially viable occupation. So a Chinese major was chosen at Plant College. Darby immediately fell in love with this small private school However, her reckless facetious remarks created a sharp dichotomy between friends and enemies; there were no in-betweens. She would mature into a formidable woman.

When friends teased Jack about the expense of Plant College, he joked: "I hate to see my loved ones leave home. I also miss my fives, tens, and twenties."

After Jack left for the city on Sunday nights and on other weeknights, Darby sneaked into the guest bedroom. Once, Derek had to muffle a moan. Afterwards, she crept back to her room.

Chapter 4: St. Bridget's and Houghton Square

The Connerty home was located blocks away from Houghton Square. It was sturdy enough to withstand everything but fire, and covered with ivy. So many interior alterations had been made over two centuries that it was difficult to tell where they started and ended.

"How many rooms?" asked Derek.

"I don't know," Darby replied, annoyed with herself for lacking an answer. He noticed two floors, a rented basement, a picket fence, and off-street parking. While waiting for Mass, Jack couldn't resist a joke about confession:

> The church was jammed. Father O'Malley was beside himself When Patrick McVey carne from confession, the priest said, "Look you're always here. You're not a big problem unless you've committed murder since the last time. You haven't, have you?
>
> McVey shook his head and started out. At the door he met Dennis McNulty and said, "You might as well go home. He's only hearing murder cases today!"

Jack asked, "Derek, why don't you accompany us?" Derek was nominally Church of England, but open-minded, and not terribly religious so he agreed.

Jack's entourage crossed the streets to white-steepled, blush-colored St. Bridget's, a handsome Catholic structure with an overhead semi-circular structural niche to protect exiting parishioners from rain.

On the sidewalk after Mass, Jack told the history of the Square. "The town was settled in 1654, but the village wasn't settled until about 100 years later. It was called Houghton Point and used for pasture. The commercial district was supposed to be built on Indian Point, on the opposite side of the cove, but Houghton Point had deeper water. In 1801, the village incorporated. Sealing and whaling brought enormous wealth. The railroad terminus from Providence arrived in 1837 and the Houghton Hotel accommodated passengers, who were waiting for steamboats to New York City. But after the railroad was connected to Morton in 1859, the hotel fell into disuse and was torn down in 1893. The new library opened in the Park about 15 years later.

Derek glanced around, "It looks like a small college campus, or an upscale city park. It has tall trees, crisscrossing sidewalks, bike racks, and benches at the corners.

Jack added, "It also has gorgeous breccia columns, inside and out; light orange and white bricks outside; and the original iron doors at the entrance."

INTERRUPTIONS IN LIFE

Chapter 5: Jeanne Connerty / Soup Kitchen:

Jeanne was volunteering at a nearby Soup Kitchen that evening. Derek was sympathetic, curious, and not at all lazy so he asked to go.

"I'd like to take you," Jeanne said. "It will be an eye-opener." She shared Jesus' message: "Do you remember the stories of Martha, Mary, and Jesus in the Bible?"

[38] Now as they went on their way, he entered a certain village, where a woman named Martha welcomed him into her home. She had a sister named Mary, who sat at the Lord's feet and listened to what he was saying. But Martha was distracted by her many tasks; so she came to him and asked, "Lord, do you not care that my sister has left me to do all the work by myself? Tell her then to help me." But the Lord answered her, "Martha, Martha, you are worried and distracted by many things; there is need of only one thing. Mary has chosen the better part, which will not be taken away from her." (Luke 10)

After the kitchen closed, Betty, tonight's director,

asked Derek: "What's your opinion of this operation?"

Derek paused. "I can't believe how many poor whites attended. And this is supposedly a rich state in a rich country. Something's not right. The food was tasty. The homeless ate as many servings as possible. One commented that he should sign up with a shelter before it gets cold, but he wanted to smoke and drink as long as possible. Do they smoke marijuana out back?"

Betty, an observant woman, remarked, "Yes, there are cheaters, but more and more poor are living on the margin and inflation will push them unto the welfare rolls."

"Can I come again?" Derek asked.

"You're a good worker. We'd love to have you."

Hardworking Jeanne was often compared to Martha in the New Testament. Although her efforts were taken for granted by her parents, Derek kidded, "I can't keep up to you."

Jeanne Connerty looked like her mother when Mary was young: buxom, black eyes, and long black hair that she liked to French braid. Jeanne was a year and a half younger than Darby. She was in her last year of high school. Although an inch shorter, she was athletic, too, and liked everything about life. She was wrapped in the youthful sack of innocence.

Derek loved to watch the feminine way she flipped strands of shiny black hair over her shoulder.

Her favorite Biblical passage was Ecclesiastes 1-3 for its joy of life. At first, Derek teased her, nicknaming her, Jeanne d'Houghton," then shortened it to "Jeanne d'Huff' because the name harkened back to Jeanne d' Arc, a French saint. She lacked a quick response, but smiled broadly. As a second child, she devoured attention. Compared to Darby, she was quieter, more religious, wore muted colors, and was conscious of the growing gap between rich and poor. Although pretty and rich, she did more than her share of work at home and at the Sunday soup kitchen.

Although her parents took Jeanne's efforts for granted, they were noticed by others, including Derek, who volunteered again to go to the Soup Kitchen.

After several strong nudges by Jack and Mary, Derek changed his travel plans by eliminating one of the stops. His superior took an extended funeral leave to Scotland so Jack didn't provide a report. It opened up a large vista on his calendar, enabling a closer look at the village and its women.

Chapter 6: Dartmouth, county Devon, England; and a Map

At noon on Sunday, before leaving with Jeanne, Mary asked "You haven't told us about your town. What does Dartmouth and Devon look like?"

"I'll give you a sketch. Dartmouth is an ancient seafaring town in the county of Devon on the western bank of the long Dart River estuary that narrows as it runs inland. Dartmouth was a deep water port and the sailing point for two crusades. Warfleet Creek was named for the vast fleets that assembled here. Dartmouth was surprised and sacked twice during the 100 year-war with France (1337-1453); afterward, a heavy chain closed the mouth of the estuary at night. Two castles were built to protect it. It's been the home of my school, the Royal Naval Academy, ever since Edward III (1312-1377). Chaucer mentions it in his *Canterbury Tales*. Smith Street was recorded in the 13th century; 16th century houses were rebuilt on the sites of medieval buildings. It was named after the smiths and shipwrights who worked here.

St. Saviour's church was consecrated in 1372. A large iron door is possibly the original. The gallery is decorated with crests and constructed with timber from a captured Armada ship (1588). Dartmouth sent many ships to the fleet that attacked the Armada. One Spanish vessel was moored here for a year and its crew had to build Greenway Estate for Sir Humphrey Gilbert and Sir Walter Raleigh. Later Agatha Christie lived there.

In 1592, a captured Portuguese treasure ship docked in Dartmouth that had so many visitors that the treasure diminished to a fourth of the original before Sir Walter Raleigh arrived to claim the throne's share.

Explorer Henry Hudson was arrested here. And your Pilgrim fathers landed before heading for America. Many medieval and Elizabethan streetscapes, lanes, and stone stairways exist. An embankment which extends along the riverfront was built in the 19th century by Napoleonic prisoners. Thomas Newcomen, the inventor of the first successful pumping machine; actress Rachel Kempson, the mother of the famous Redgraves; and Christopher Robin Milne (character for Winnie-the-

Pooh books) lived here.

It's an ancient borough of three parishes, that has diminished in importance over time. The present population is around 5000. It's on the English Channel, near Plymouth, and 380 km southwest of London .. The red cliffs, a royal regatta, boat cruises, medieval villages, two castles, a maritime museum, marshlands, and salt air draw tourists. Bayard's Cove has been used for TV. Devon has three vast foggy moors.

Mary inquired, "You mentioned the Armada many times. In school, we glossed over the subject too quickly. Tell us about it."

"Philip II of Spain decided to invade England, overthrow Elizabeth, reestablish Catholicism, and stop English interference in the Netherlands and with shipping. Beforehand, Francis Drake made a raid on Cadiz that delayed Spanish preparations.

In late May, 1588, an Armada of 130 ships began sailing to the Spanish Netherlands to escort barges of invading troops. On July 19th, signal beacons burned along the coast to alert the English of the approach. The inexperienced new Spanish commander chose not to attack the English at Plymouth or Portsmouth. In the first encounter two Spanish ships were lost because of a collision. The Spanish anchored off Calais. On the 23rd another engagement took place. At midnight on the 28th, the closely anchored Armada was scattered by an English fireship attack. Next day, at the Battle of Gravelines, (off Flanders) five Spanish ships were sunk and many more badly damaged. Unable to join their army by shoals and a fleet of small Dutch ships, and disheartened, they avoided more encounters by sailing around the British Isles. Because storms and the drift of the Gulf Stream interfered with navigation, they ventured too close to Ireland and many shipwrecks occurred.

All told, one-third of the Armada was lost (35 ships and 20,000 dead) . The English fleet actually outnumbered the Spanish (200 to 130) but had fewer guns and supplies, including gunpowder. Our ships were faster and more maneuverable, that along with the better seamanship of our 'seadogs' avoided Spanish-type grappling and bombarded at a distance. Technology made a difference. The English fleet became the best in the world."

INTERRUPTIONS IN LIFE

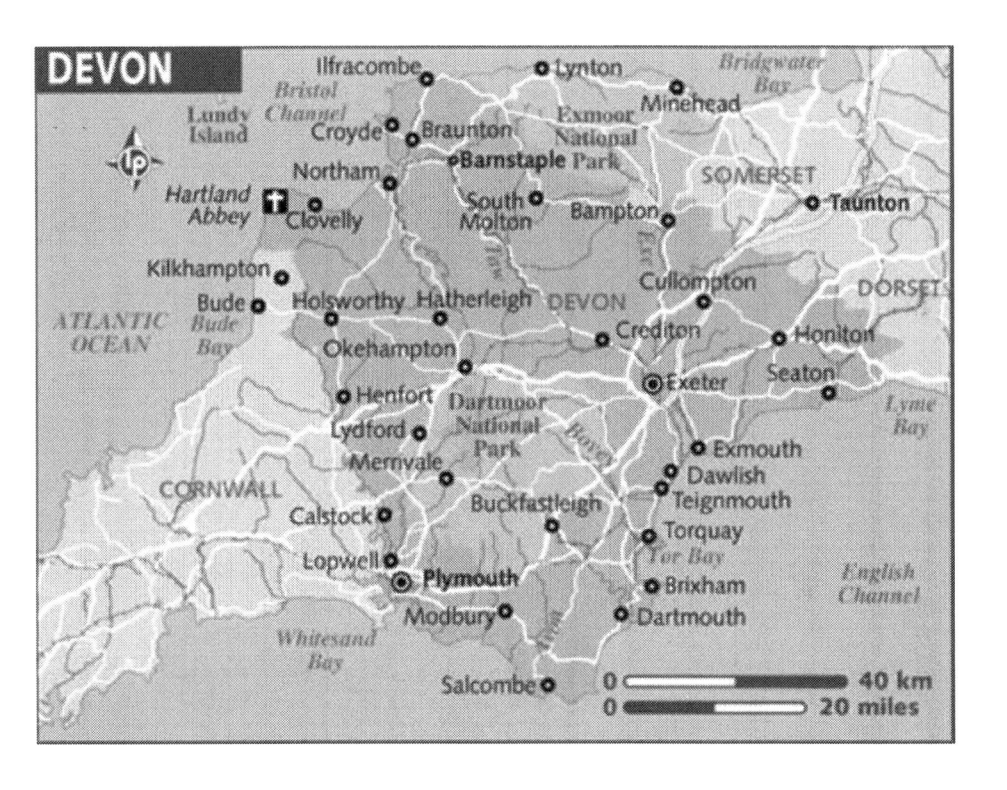

INTERRUPTIONS IN LIFE

Chapter 7: Houghton Village

"Now your turn, what's unique about Haughton? It's confusing: Is it Houghton Town, Village, or District? Sounds like the nursery rhyme, *Going to St. Ives*?"

> "As I was going to St. Ives
> I met a man with seven wives,
> Every wife had seven sacks,
> Every sack had seven cats,
> Every cat had seven kits—
> Kits, cats, sacks, and wives,
> How many were going to St. Ives?"

Jeanne laughed. "We live in the village, but it's also called The District. The larger political entity is the Town of Houghton." Jeanne grabbed Derek's arm. "C'mon, let's go for a quick walk on the two principal streets, Garver and Warren."

Darby's jaw dropped! Her competition was her own sister. From now on, the Connerty sisters quarreled bitterly. Although Darby was quick-witted, loud, and more sarcastic, Jeanne could "strike to the quick," and today was unruffled, ignoring the insults, and explained the history of the village.

"Although the Old Custom House is still there and the Catholic Society is open, most of Garver Street is residential. We'll cross in front of the cannons that defended Houghton from the British. Behind the factory-like condos are luxurious separate waterfront condos. At the end of the internal green is a renovated foundry called the LaGrua Center that's used for music, lectures and classes. The Point, itself, has parking and a beach." Derek was admiring the seascape, but Jeanne said, "Let's go—we've got to get to the soup kitchen."

During the next week, while the girls were away at a wedding, Derek explored, walking south to the cannons and Houghton Point. Residents walking dogs or sweeping leaves proudly gave directions. The revolutionary and Federal era houses were handsome and well kept. Midway, the Catholic society, with its canopy, multiple flags, and sign, was the most colorful. A few houses used accent colors. Derek noticed that lots of money had been spent on restoration. One house had more than ten filigreed porch columns and others had unique iron fences. A plaque on a boulder commemorated the 1837 inception of railroad traffic to Providence. One woman said that after several moves, the oldest house in the village was now at Hickcock and Garver. There's an old Baptist Church on a cross street. On Garver Street, large gold stars marked prestigious dwellings. Lots of painters and poets come to Houghton.

INTERRUPTIONS IN LIFE

Chapter 8: Walking on Warren Street

Warren Street is commercial, but quaint and leads to Houghton Point. The alleyways and side streets have a European flair. "One's first impression," Jeanne said, "is that the village is loaded with 'snotty' people, but they loosen up. It's a fun place. It's turning into a vibrant intellectual center. Lectures are held at two locations. Real estate, antique shops, boutiques, restaurants, and coffee houses took over the spaces that formerly provided residential services.

"Some of the restaurants are on the harbor; all of them are great. "Mates's Dock" is noteworthy because it catches boating activity as the sun sets in the west over Indian Point; no one wants to leave and long lines form. They like to watch boats, like that one with the limp mainsail that's motoring to its mooring. A launch will take them to Matson's Boatyard; then they'll decide where to eat. There's hundreds of sail and powerboats in the cove. For new visitors, this is where the seascape opens up. The museum on Warren Street always has an interesting display. The owner of the Blue house at the point used to put fake Halloween tombstones next to the sidewalk. The 'last words' that he composed were hilarious."

"You'd love the English village of Clovelly;" Derek said. "It's so dramatic —calendars show the town cascading down stones to the waterfront. Not far is Bayard's Cove, a popular cobblestoned half-timbered neighborhood." "Let's have tea? Along with thatch, we have cream teas in Devon—It's so civilized." Talking with Jeanne put him completely at ease. After learning bird identification, he began calling her "My little Chickadee." And she talked so freely.

"Because of Federal restrictions, the commercial fishing fleet is down to less than a dozen boats. Many fishermen have sold out. As the old-timers died, their houses were bought by out-of-towners. In addition, two mills have closed; many workers have left, also. The village is gentrifying rapidly. Debby beach is perfect for kids. Many present and former residents greet sunrise at Houghton Point in pickups with mugs of coffee. Beyond the breakwaters is Fishers Island Sound. What a delightful mélange." She pointed, "Midway across the street is the boyhood home of a 20-year-old explorer. Soon, I'll show you the interior of the mansion that he built for his wife. We already passed it. Did you notice the three gorgeous federals across the square with Gingko trees that have turned bright, Jasmine gold."

"Jeanne," Derek said, kissing her ear, "Except for the moors, Houghton feels more like my Dartmouth than anywhere else in America." Jeanne impulsively kissed him on the cheek.

"You're more like my man than anyone else in America!" It belied her shy reputation. Derek was impressed. "I can see why Connecticut has become a tourist and retirement Mecca. For me, the views and marinas are fascinating." (and especially the women.)

INTERRUPTIONS IN LIFE

Chapter 9: Noon at the Historical Society; the Moors

Derek teased Jeanne: "The Irish talk about wee people. Do they have kidney problems? On the second Saturday in July, Jeanne suggested to Derek, "Let's walk to the Historical Society; there's a wonderful spot on the Cove that I want to show you."

Joggers passed them as they crossed the railroad tracks. Jeanne and Derek made two turns and found the street on the left. Quarried stone walls lined both sides. A path led through the brush on the cove side of the Historical Society, and wound around to a quiet bench overlooking a cove.

"Let's relax for a spell," said Derek. "Parts of the village: the houses, coves, rocks, and marshes remind me of Devon. Can you access the ocean from here?"

"Only if the boat has a low freeboard or at low tide. Access will continue to be bad until Amtrak replaces the two bridges with ones that provide higher clearances.

"Crossing the tracks, you pointed out a large boatyard with a "forest" of masts."

"That's Matson's. Not the biggest marina but an extremely profitable one." Jeanne said. "My family is frequently invited on cruises around Long Island Sound or to the islands."

"What islands?"

"Martha's Vineyard, Nantucket, Block, Shelter Island, Gardiners, and even the Hamptons from a marina on Montauk Point."

"What kind of ducks are over there?" asked Derek, pointing across the cove.

"Without a glass, I can't identify them."

" Is that Route-1 on the north side?"

"Yes," said Jeanne. "West, it goes to Morton, the Subase, and Coast Guard Academy. East, the road goes to Rhode Island."

Derek had an incident to tell: "A few residents are weary of questions. During the week that I walked around the village, I asked a woman sweeping leaves in front of the former Baptist Church, "Who lives in the church now?"

"Do you know that dark Blue house near the point? Ask that guy; he owns it!"

"But to be fair, the village is very well preserved—everyone is so proud."

Sitting on the bench, with the wind rustling the brush, leaves flapping overhead, and the water lapping the shore, made it as peaceful and relaxing as the lost world of Shangri-La in James Hilton's *Lost Horizon.*

Jeanne broke the spell with her schoolgirl's obsession for Sherlock Holmes, "Tell me about the moors?" Derek had often walked on the moors: "The closest one to my town is Dartmoor National Park, a 954 square km ragged oval, northeast of Plymouth. It has furze, (a grass), granite tors (hilltops with boulder-like formations) heathery valleys, and bogs. The highest point is High Willhays, over 621 m, (2037 feet) above sea level. More than 160 hilltops have "tors" in their names. They are the focus of the annual "Ten Tors challenge," when about 2400 people walk for days between ten tors on different routes.

Dartmoor includes the largest area of granite in Britain, most of it under superficial peat. It was intruded into sedimentary Carboniferous rocks 300 million years ago.

The moor takes its name from the Dart river. More rain falls in the park than surrounding areas. Its thick peat absorbs rain quickly and distributes it slowly. Where water accumulates, dangerous bogs topped by moss are formed, called "feather beds" or "quakers" because they quake underfoot. Fox Tor Mires is notorious for one in Doyle's *The Hound of the Baskervilles.* The weather in Southwest England is the most temperate in Britain. Snowfall is uncommon.

Prehistory dates back to the Late Neolithic and early Bronze age. It has the largest concentration of remains in Britain. The climate was warmer then and most of the moors were covered by trees. Settlers burned the land to create pasture and farmland. Periodic burning expanded the moors, but acidified the soil, and peat and bogs accumulated. Climate change made this area uninhabitable.

Numerous standing stones, stone circles, kistvaens (Neolithic, stone, box-like tombs,) cairns, and multiple stone rows exist. Remnants of Bronze Age houses, from 6 feet to 30 feet wide, probably with conical, turf or thatch-covered roofs, remain. The earliest surviving farms, from the 14th century, are known as the Ancient Tenements. This moor has the marks of centuries, such as Dartmoor prison, tin mining, the military, and abandoned farmhouses.

It's known for its legends: pixies, headless horseman, spectral hounds, a large black dog, and even a visit by the devil. Landmarks such as graves, rock piles, and stone crosses have legends and ghost stories associated with them, inspiring many writers. J. K. Rowling included a competition on the moor in *Harry Potter and the Goblet of Fire.*

The Park is different than others, because it's 57% privately owned and mostly designated as "access land." Though private, walkers are allowed to roam.

INTERRUPTIONS IN LIFE

Chapter 10: Derek's Family

Back home, Jack had arrived from New York. He worked as a partner at an investment firm close to Penn Station. It was much quicker to take the train than to suffer weekend tie-ups on I-95. And in the long run just as cheap. Jack left for the city on Sunday nights and returned on Friday.

He asked, "What about your family? You haven't mentioned them at all."

"I have two brothers and a sister. I'm the oldest. We live in a small house in Dartmouth with tiny rooms and one loo. Your house is a castle compared to ours. Like Philip Schultz, the poet we heard last week, my mom and dad were failures as greengrocers. Business got worse and worse. Now they're clerking for someone else.

"If I wasn't accepted at the Royal Naval Academy in Dartmouth, I wouldn't have gone to college at all. My brothers and sister are trying to sort things out and find careers. I haven't talked to them lately."

In the morning when Derek awoke, Jeanne was snuggled against his shoulder.

"Derek, I'm no competition for Darby, but can I just snuggle here for a moment and dream?"

He slid his hand down her chest; but she clasped it and moved it back. "Caught ya," she giggled. He laughed. Differences in the two sisters were obvious. He didn't dare call it "night and day," but Jeanne's big breasts really turned him on.

Derek felt her warmth against his side in the coolness of the morning. He daydreamed about the choice he must make; laughing to himself, "Why do I have to make a choice? I'm already getting everything!"

"Let's walk today, okay?"

They heard morning noises upstairs. "Did Mom hear us?"

Jeanne quietly hopped to her bedroom, but returned several mornings a week.

Chapter 11: Tom Sherrill

Jack Connerty was tall, stocky, and very persuasive. From sarcasm and outright arguments in his girls' conversations, he realized the seriousness of their competition over Derek. He thought he'd better get involved, to get to know this young man.

He called Mary from New York, who said the girls had another quarrel this morning. Jack's boss gave him permission to leave early. He called again.

"Can Derek pick me up at 3 pm at the Train Station? Please give him directions!"

While Derek was driving home, Jack said: "I want to show you a piece of Americana.

Turn left here and left again and enter Houghton Cemetery." They walked to the "poets' corner" where the graves of Pulitzer Prize winning poet Tom Sherrill and his partner Dan are marked with simple elegance.

"This isn't a new cemetery—it's very rustic! Sherrill's site has beds of moss under black oaks. His stone is old-fashioned and very artistic. Above Sherrill's name is a blazing sun, waning moon, and two morning stars (or planets?) It's believed to represent life, death and the two partners. Some theorize Sherrill was referring to a Biblical passage in Job." Jack pondered; "They're right—he loved symbols:"

> Or who stretched the line upon it?
> On what were its bases sunk?
> Or who laid its cornerstone
> When the morning stars sang together
> And all the heavenly beings shouted for joy?
> (Job 38: 4-7)

"In front of Sherrill's is a large mausoleum. Sherrill's choice is simpler and more artistic? Much better than his poetry. The bigger mausoleum was built by a heartsick couple. It's falling apart. I went to the Library to copy an early poem by Sherrill to show how simple life was in the '60s."

INTERRUPTIONS IN LIFE

The Summer People

" . . . et l'hiver resterait la saison intellectuelle créatrice."

Mallarmé

On our New England coast was once
A village white and neat
With Greek Revival houses,
Sailboats, a fishing fleet,

Two churches and two liquor stores,
An Inn, a Gourmet Shoppe,
A library, a pharmacy.
Trains passed but did not stop.

Gold Street was rich in neon,
Main Street in rustling trees
Untouched as yet by hurricanes
And the Dutch elm disease.

On Main the summer people
Took deep-rooted ease—
A leaf turned red, to town they'd head.
On Gold lived the Portuguese

Whose forebears had manned whalers.
Two years from the Azores
Saw you with ten gold dollars
Upon these fabled shores.

Feet still pace the whaler's deck

At the Caustic (Me.) Museum.
A small stuffed whale hangs overhead
As in the head a dream.

Slowly the fleet was shrinking.
The good-sized fish were few.
Town meetings closed and opened
With the question what to do.

"Soon literature got really complicated; especially Sherrill's poetry. Please scan it and tell me what you think. Philip Schultz's tragic poem, *The One Truth*—is much more understandable."

"This is one of the turning points in your life. You're quiet and smart. My daughters see something in you. I agree. You would do terrific on one of our trading desks for ten years and then become a financial manager. Needless to say, it's very lucrative.

The girls began descending the staircase.

"Tell the girls we talked about sports; don't mention careers!" Jack ordered and started talking about the Red Sox and Patriots; and Derek, Manchester United.

"Okay, Pop." Derek hesitated."

    "Don't call me pop! Call me Dad," insisted Jack. "Here's the really definitive word on advice:"

Panicked by a letter telling him that an IRS
Audit is upcoming, a man calls his accountant,
Who responds, "Don't worry. I have all the bills
And papers. I've got every receipt. But let me give
You one word of caution. When you show up
There, dress like a derelict—torn jacket, torn shirt,
old shoes. If the auditor sees you're poor, he won't
come down hard on you."
Still concerned, the man phones his attorney and
Explains the situation. The attorney says, "I'm sure
Your accountant had everything under control. You'll
do fine. But one thing—dress well. The auditor will see
that you look nice, you're respectable, and obviously a
man of responsibility. Surely you wouldn't lie on your
tax returns. He'll give you a break.
More mixed up than ever, the man goes to his minister
And again explains the difficult problem. The minister
says, I have the same problem with marriages.
The mother of the bride wants her to dress like an

old-fashioned girl. She wants her daughter to look nice on her honeymoon, but not wild enough to bring out the beast in her groom. The bride's father wants her to be provocative. He wants her to wear something revealing. I tell the bride, "What you wear doesn't matter. You're going to get screwed!"

Chapter 12: HMS Dauntless

Derek was opportunistic. He pursued the opportunity for free schooling at the Royal Naval Academy at Dartmouth in Devon. "No flies on him," said Jack.

While driving to the mall on Sunday, Jeanne asked, "How many other ships have been named, "Dauntless?"

"Three other ships, a land station, and a plane have carried the same name as my ship, the "HMS Dauntless." The best example is the American dive-bomber, 'Dauntless,' that caught the Japs refueling and broke the back of the Japanese fleet at Midway."

Jeanne said, "My Uncle Dylan flew a "Dauntless" at the end of the war in the Pacific, but he never talks about it."

"The guys that returned hardly ever did. Soon, I'll be deployed on a Dauntless. Here's my ship."

INTERRUPTIONS IN LIFE

INTERRUPTIONS IN LIFE

Chapter 13: Darby's Despair

Although preparations for a trip to Chinatown had only started a month ago, Darby had already found worldly-wise pals. When she agonized that she wanted to catch this trophy, they laughed and gave a simple answer: "Screw the living brains out of him—he'll come around!"

For Darby, it was depressing to think she could lose Derek. Her vibrant personality became dispirited and she made cruel remarks to Jeanne. Her prey was handsome and the alliteration of names (Derek/Darby) was unique, magical; and somewhat spooky.

When not so naïve Mary asked, "Why are you home? You were just here days ago."

"Mom, I have to concentrate on a special project." At night, she climbed into Derek's bed and banged away until exhausted. Derek didn't object, he was willing, but Darby sensed a new mood.

INTERRUPTIONS IN LIFE

Chapter 14: An Injury

A crucial injury happened on the fourth Friday in July. Derek went dancing with Jeanne, Darby, and two classmates. They danced until midnight. Derek had his hands too full with the four women. They lined up three big glasses of "Sam Adams" in front of him. Sometimes only Derek and one of his harem were dancing.

On Saturday at 9 a.m., Derek woke up late, wiped out after two nights of drinking, nights of dancing and sex, and a long daytime hike. The bedside lamp was on all night. His right shoulder ached. Last night's feverish dancing had aggravated a teenage injury. Was it reinjured by the frantic arm swinging of the twist?

The condition of his shoulder worsened. Sunday morning, it ached so bad that Derek couldn't put on a short sleeve undershirt. He couldn't reach across the desk to answer the phone.

After Monday calls to the Subase, The Royal Naval Academy, and Veteran's Affairs, a local resident examined his right shoulder. The small rotator cuff muscles were reinjured by the strenuous weekend dancing.

INTERRUPTIONS IN LIFE

Derek drove with his left arm. An appointment was made with a VA orthopedist on Tuesday.

Wednesday morning, the painkiller made Derek sleep until 10 a.m. He considered stopping it—he had things to do. He complained to Jeanne: "I go to bed with shoulder pain, I wake up with pain. Every night is a torture chamber. I'm not getting restful sleep—only 3-4 hours at best. I can remember when it was a pleasure to wake up refreshed in the morning. No longer! I've tried one home remedy after another. Nothing works. My optimistic outlook has disappeared into bouts of melancholy."

Tony, Jack's livery driver, came in to say hello. He was veteran of Korea who had had lots of pain. He told Derek to take the painkiller every day or face possible serious consequences. Derek followed his advice.

Jeanne drove Derek to VA West Haven. Derek asked the orthopedist, "What can be done other than surgery?" The doctor restored his confidence, "There's a ninety percent chance of recovery by using therapy."

Therapy started the next day. With a week,

Derek's shoulder showed enormous improvement. The pain was minimal by early August.

INTERRUPTIONS IN LIFE

Chapter 15: Mary Connerty

Mary was pretty, but plump with a few remaining black highlights. She considered herself to be a well-off, old-fashioned housewife, who led a good life but lacked the refinements or intellectual experiences of college graduates. However, she made good friends at the library and church by volunteering on two weekdays.

Like most American mothers of the post-war era, Mary trained her daughters to be "modern." Although she hadn't attended college, she knew that's where successful men gathered. From their earliest years, Mary reminded her girls, "It takes two paychecks to raise a family. So start thinking about careers. College will also make you more attractive to men." She diligently prepared her girls by helping them with homework until bedtime. Mary sparked Darby's interest in Chinese, but still hadn't found a career for Jeanne.

Though she was a heavy sleeper, Mary wasn't stupid as some might think, and was very aware of the goings on. At first, it was completely overwhelming; she never comprehended how loose and open modern premarital sex would be. Almost belatedly, she warned her girls to take precautions: "You can catch a man with sex, but you might catch a lot more, too."

But the arguments turned bitter, beyond benevolence, and made her realize that she was taking an awful risk of losing the girls and driving them away. She finally decided: enough was enough! She wouldn't be able to control their entire lives; nor should she try. Let them live their own lives. We brought them up to be independent. They don't want advice—so don't give it. The girls would have to sort things out by themselves. If they asked, she would respond.

Chapter 16: Jeanne d'Arc

Every Sunday was different at the soup kitchen. Tonight, plenty of help showed up. His right shoulder was improved, but Derek lifted left handed.

Joan was a pleasant, soft-spoken, disabled worker at the soup kitchen to whom many retirees would be attracted. She was too old for Derek, but perhaps, a delightful catch for one of Jeanne's uncles. The following week Jeanne introduced uncle Dylan to Joan by saying, "Joan gives the best back rubs."

"That's the ticket!" enthused Dylan.

Faithful Jeanne's personality and hard work turned many heads. They teased her,

"You're more like a soldier, more like Jeanne d' Arc!" She laughed at them. In her heart, Jeanne knew she was just an ordinary girl doing the best she could.

But Derek thought she was special, his Jeanne D' Arc. Since Derek teased her so much, it was only right to learn about her namesake "Joan of Arc," who was born at Domremy in NE France during the 100 Years

War. The French were decimated by multiple plagues, civil war, famine, and brigands (marauders).

At 13, in 1425, Joan saw a bright light and heard the voice of St. Michael. At first, the voice said "Believe, Be Good, Go to Church." Next, the visions included St. Catherine and St. Margaret "Go to France," i.e. go to the aid of Charles VIII to end the French Civil War and oust the English. Joan had only the training of a peasant (tending animals and spinning). Brigands roamed.

A 19-year old girl soldier, she rode to relieve the siege of Orleans. Joan was a virgin, who was known as "Jeanne la Pucelle," "Joan the Maid," or simply "The Maid." Not until 1576, was "Joan of Arc" used.

Mary Gordon wrote "There is no one like her." And "She was palpably in the company of the Divine." Joan was ascetic in sex, food, hard physical activity, stress, and had a down to earth personality. Mary Gordon believed this was her undoing.

Captured in 1430, she tried in Rouen for 3 months. On May 30, 1431, Joan was burned as a heretic.

Cardinal Beaufort ordered Joan's ashes to be thrown into the Seine River.

Why was Joan burned and not Hildegaard von Bingen (1098-1179), who also experienced visions and lights, and gave advice to important people? According to Gordon, Joan is the 3rd most popular artistic subject: Voltaire (Maid of Orlean); George Bernard Shaw (St. Jean); Friedrich Schiller (The Maid of Orleans); Shakespeare (Henry IV part I); and Mark Twain (Personal Recollections of Joan of Arc).

INTERRUPTIONS IN LIFE

Chapter 17: The Economy

Even before the 2008 election, it was apparent that the economy was badly broken, almost ruined. Ballooning credit had kept up the appearances of prosperity. Panics and depressions have happened in the past, right under the noses of prominent financial figures. During supper, Jack lectured, "How do we get out from under the crap that successive presidents have buried us under?"

"I'll tell you how! MANAGE the budget. SUSPEND imports of electronics gear. REDUCE inflation. CEASE meddling in overseas affairs. BUILD up our economy instead of burying it. RESCIND the tax cuts for the rich. Despite free trade treaties, BRING BACK some mercantilism, REDUCE the exorbitant salaries and perks of CEOs. BRING BACK Robert Rubin to the treasury. STOP the shenanigans!"

Jeanne spoke up: "A great man wrote, 'A man is rich in proportion to the number of things which he can afford to let alone.' I don't need luxuries; none of us do!"

"What do call a luxury?" Darby asked.

Jack broke in, "Mary, remember the Depression song, *Hallelujah I'm a Bum!*" Everyone joined in:

> Hallelujah ! I'm a bum,
> Hallelujah bum again,
> Hallelujah! Give a handout
> To revive us again.
>
> Oh why don't you work
> like other men do?
> How the hell can I work
> When the skies are so blue?
>
> Oh, I like my boss.
> He's a good friend of mine,
> And that's why I'm standing
> Out in the breadline.
> (John Husband)

Privately, Jack and Mary wondered whether this generation could endure another Depression?

Chapter 18: Morton Point

Jeanne was confused about a major and contemplated taking a year off, but her parents motivated her to keep up with Darby. First, Jeanne drove to UConn—Morton Point on the beautiful Morton shoreline, and then visited other schools, as well.

On her first visit, a vermillion border ringed the entire horizon. On the second, strings of post-sunset stratus clouds looked like islands in the sky. On another, a schooner with beautiful burgundy and yellow striped sails left the adjoining Yacht Club and passed through the narrow Pine Island channel. It wheeled around and passed in the opposite direction. But the most obvious "sign," a page-boy "bluff" of soft yellow/white clouds curled under far to the south with a closer bank of rosy-white ones right-angled north, all punctuated by a spiky steel gray ocean surface.

The omens were spectacular and Jeanne enthusiastically acknowledged them. For the following year, she picked an "American Studies" major at UConn-Morton Point, preparing to study history and obtain a teaching degree.

Chapter 19: Decision Time for Derek

Of course, the inevitable call from the Royal Naval Academy came the second week of August. After returning from funeral leave to Scotland, Derek's C.O. noticed that no reports came from Derek. So he checked at the Subase.

By the time he reached Derek, he was furious and bellowed, "What in the world are you doing? Setting up a house of Bigamy? You're AWOL. Do you want to continue in the Royal Navy? Then return in three days! Period! Do you understand? Otherwise, the Yanks will jail you." Derek didn't try to explain because had disobeyed orders. He was in a delicate position and had to return to school. His career was over, but for these weeks, he had never felt so welcome in his life. He wanted, and he felt the Connerty's wanted, for him to join them. But which sister?

Darby was beautiful, brilliant, but overbearing. She would be formidable and use him like "Chinese checkers," advancing a marble on the board of life. Sex with her was great, but in ten years? Could he trust her? She would be torture in married life.

He didn't agonize over this decision. Everything was apparent. He knew he had someone that was faithful, patient, quiet, good with kids, and a partner for life. Derek had come to love Jeanne's quiet competent ways. Not only were her views on expensive hairdos and clothes different from other women, but her personality and outlook on life were compatible with his own. He loved his black and white "chickadee" and spent as much time as possible with her, because she was fun to be with. He could talk with her without sensing competition.

Jack followed Spinoza's Proposition 37: man's desire to have others rejoice in the good in which he rejoices, not to make others live according to his thinking. Derek asked Jack to walk.

"Let's go to Sherrill's former 3rd floor apartment on Warren Street," Jack suggested.

Standing in front, Jack explained: "Sherrill died of a heart attack from AIDS. He won many poetry prizes. The plaque is tasteful: "Tom Sherrill…American Poet…Lived here."

Very Plain and Simple! His erudite gentleness, aided for 25 years by his spirit "Ezekiel" and his partner Dan, increased his fame. But a lone critic wrote, 'The reader may not understand the 'in jokes.' Isn't that the truth!"

"I found them indecipherable." Derek said. Jack paused, "Few people want to decipher them and Sherrill's gone to the cosmos. So the message is, 'Life and fame are fleeting.' There's an easily penetrated membrane between existence and eternity." "Perhaps you remember this line from *Herzog*? 'But I am still on the same side of eternity as ever' That's his fine line, his struggle. For us, the line is the one between love and hate. Marriages like Virginia Woolf's are like war. So finish your naval commitment and marry the girl you're comfortable with. I'll help; but the choice is yours!"

INTERRUPTIONS IN LIFE

Chapter 20: Epilogue—Four Years Later

After graduation Jeanne will marry Derek on the prairie-like oceanfront lawn of the Morton House at Morton Point. After the honeymoon, she'll be a financial courier, traveling around the world for Jack.

Derek is trading stocks in Jack's new firm on Wall Street, learning the business from the ground up.

Darby has set-up a Shanghai Office for booming Asian sales—She'll be its Director. Perhaps, Orientals can tolerate her verbal onslaughts.

Mary still patiently waits for a grandchild.

Jack continues to spin jokes:

"I'm confused. The national anthem tells us that this is the land of the free.
My accountant tells me it isn't."

"I have a CPA who's brilliant. They named a loop-hole after him."

"Old accountants never die. They just lose their balances."

INTERRUPTIONS IN LIFE

Sources:

Morton Public Library

Joan of Arc: The Legend and the Reality, Frances Geis

Failure, by Philip Schultz

Hallelujah! I'm a Bum, John Husband

Milton Berle's Private Joke File, Milton Berle

Internet, Google, MSN, Wikipedia

Superintendent of the Houghton Cemetery

Joan of Arc, M. Gordon

Houghton Chronology, William Hagnes

Contemporary Authors, New Revision Series, Vol. 108

From the First Nine: Poems 1946-1976, Tom Sherrill

Frommer's England 2007

National Geographic Trends, Great Britain

Herzog, Saul Bellow

Soup Kitchen

NRSV of the *Holy Bible*

Houghton Historical Society

England and Wales, ed. by J. Norwich

Lost Horizons, James Hilton

Map of Devon, Internet

INTERRUPTIONS IN LIFE

Shad Point:
The Belated Advent of Love

A Novella

Bernard D. Boylan

2008, 2015, 2017

INTERRUPTIONS IN LIFE

Preface:

The Wildlife Management Area at Shad Point is a region of short points and wide marshes on the coast of Connecticut. The point, itself, is on the Liberty River that drains most of southern Rhode Island and parts of Connecticut. Before mills and dams were built upstream, large seines were deployed in the river to harvest the spring spawning of shad, salmon, and alewives. American Shad are silvery with a greenish-blue back; and a dark spot behind the gill cover with smaller spots behind. Adults are usually 20 inches long and weight 12 pounds. Pools of shad run up rivers to spawn.

Before the Industrial Age, they were an important fish. Although their numbers have recently been regular, they are vastly depleted because of dams and pollution. Selections from the report of the U.S. Commissioner of Fish and Fisheries in 1898 explain the catastrophic drop in the quantity of shad. Pages 259 and 260 state that the Liberty River formerly yielded a "large" number of shad.

Wouldn't it have been fun, 150 years ago, to live

on well-named Shad Point during the spring run and catch fish to your heart's content?

In former years, another valuable food source at Shad Point was salt hay from marshes, an important source of food and bedding for cattle and horses, and sustenance for large numbers of shorebirds.

Special thanks to the reference librarians in Westerly and Groton, to Maggie from the Nature Center, to Lois Pazienza, to deceased Tom from the Singles Group who showed me the trails, and to the fishermen in my extended family: Jim, Jay, and Bill.

Table of Contents............................*Shad Point*

Preface:

Chapter 1: Shad Point

Chapter 2: Philip Meets Judi

Chapter 3: Philip and Judi's Backgrounds

Chapter 4: Sculptors and Problems

Chapter 5: Philip Schultz

Chapter 6: "Egg Timer Riddle"

Chapter 7: Lafayette's Marsh

Chapter 8: The Shed and Prohibition

Chapter 9: Restoration of Marriage and Nature

Chapter 10: Dad

Epilogue: Tami

Sources

INTERRUPTIONS IN LIFE

Chapter 1: Shad Point

    This story was undertaken to identify a different type of trail. a destination for the growing number of hikers, who believe walking is beneficial to the body, mind, and soul. Although controversial, some say there's a fixed number of heartbeats in everyone's lifespan and exercise will shorten it. The reverse may be true: better-toned muscles, including the heart, may last longer. No conclusion has been reached. Perhaps both extremes (too much, too little) are bad. (See Chapter 6 for the "egg-timer riddle.")

    Years ago, still-valid explanations were given for the linkage between solitude, mental attitude, companionship, and physical health. Regular walking for 30 minutes is wildly beneficial, a tonic to the soul, and twice as enjoyable with a partner. Thoreau, a "walker, errant" thought, "I cannot preserve my health and spirits unless I spend four hours ... sauntering through the woods ... absolutely free from all worldly entanglements."

    Almost all of the women who walk at Shad Point

have a leashed dog or two, a sign of the times.

The western trailhead is at a pull-off at the crest of the access road. The eastern end in lower Liberty is another entrance/parking area. An alternate trail loop is found in the woods. All novice hikers in Eastern Connecticut will be surprised at the contrast between their woodlands of north/south ridges and the Management Area at Shad Point. Long, wide berms, interrupted only by gravel-covered culverts, with fall-blooming groundsel shrubs on either side, extend from hummocks to knolls to woods. The sense of a different world, a different ecosystem, prevails. At feeding times, snowy egrets, cormorants, herons, oystercatchers, and glossy ibises are often seen. Ospreys hover and dive.

An old cemetery is at the eastern end. Close by is the 350-year-old Davis-Stanton farmhouse! Physical Shad Point is private and a mile south of the farmhouse. On the southern side of the Park berms is a strange wild seascape of marsh and hummocks with the horizon monopolized by Fishers Island, NY, and Napatree Point, RI.

Chapter 2: Philip Meets Judi

The modern history of the Wildlife Management Area at Shad Point, CT is brief. The State began acquiring parcels in the mid-'40s and now manages over 1000 acres. The marsh was mistakenly impounded in the late '40s. In 1982, 2.1 meter-wide culverts were installed to restore tidal flushing.

***

A woman in a brown exercise outfit with dogs caught up to Philip while he was walking to the west access road. Because of broad military, school, and business experience, Philip could to talk to anyone, from privates to generals, from immigrants to CEOs. Pointing to the large brown and white spaniels, he joked, "Are they the attack dogs we read about?"

"No," she laughed. "They're really pussycats."

Philip cocked his head, smirked, and asked, "What kind of pussycat is that?"

She laughed again. "Brittany Spaniels, I love them. They were bred more for bird hunting like a pointer or setter."

Later internet research confirmed them as: Solidly built, long legs, floppy ears, intelligent, alert, elastic and free gait.

Philip kept talking, hoping to slow her down and gain a walking partner.

"I'm writing about Prohibition in this area. I call it *The Terminus.*

She slowed. "There's an ample supply of stories in this area." She thought a large shed built on the farthest hummock, "Shad Island" (formerly Stanchion Island) could have been used for shad, salt hay, and bootleg liquor. The island used to be reached by a bridge over a marsh. Kayakers could paddle underneath.

"My name is Philip. What's yours?"

She hesitated, "Judi."

Later, friends said her real name was Cori, named by her astronomer father for the

"Coriolis Effect," the apparent deflection of a body in motion.

"The weather is pretty good for late February," Philip remarked, keeping the conversation going. "It's a lot warmer than January and we haven't had much snow or ice." He hoped for the best, but realized the relationship wouldn't last. He observed a large ring. But for the moment, he was glad to have Judi to walk with; possibly, she could be a partner.

Since boyhood, Philip had most of the personality traits of his father: honesty, loyalty, and hard work. His dad always smiled until his final illness. Philip, however, was different; frowning was one of his shortcomings.

Philip wished he had classic hair like Dad, but was glad to inherit his mother's nose. He was about one inch shorter than Dad and unusually small for his generation. Better nutrition hadn't worked for him. Judi was slightly taller; was it her boots?

Unlike Dad, who wouldn't talk about issues, Philip was too forthright and had lots of opinions about politics, the church, and life. Speaking out made him feel fulfilled. By 20, his mind always demanded the truth and hated cover-ups. At 40 and established in suburbia with a considerable wake of liberal affiliations, his loyalty trait kicked-in, making him work within New England conservatism. Most of his friends had turned ultra-liberal.

Then betrayal struck in the form of divorce! By now, he had weathered it enough to talk to his ex, but the animosity of the divorce made him switch loyalties again, to those of his college years. He searched for intellectual friends and activities in town.

It was not surprising that natives were very conservative; he found himself searching at college events for friends among the faculty and attendees. He enjoyed these functions and made friends, but couldn't seem to match up with a compatible woman. Widows stuck together, or wouldn't go out alone.

Philip asked Judi, "Can I walk with you again on Friday?"

"Yes—I'll meet you here at 9:00. If I'm not here after fifteen minutes, go alone!"

***

A stranger would say Judi's face was less than

beautiful, but rather pretty. She had a pert nose with shoulder-length wavy brown hair, a welcome addition to the usual repertoire of blond/black/white colors. Judi was lanky with long legs, long strides and thin. Her public persona consisted of wholesome good health from invigorating walking; a good mother of teens in high school; and the loyal wife of a successful husband. But she stuck to herself—her friends were few.

Although she was ambitious, her determination was cooped-up in a suburban ranch that was noisy from dogs and teens. Right or wrong, during the week, she felt she couldn't attend activities in town with males because of gossip. Judi had a feminine sense of humor about her predicament: she called this her cocoon phase. Inside was a writer waiting to be born.

INTERRUPTIONS IN LIFE

Chapter 3: Philip and Judi's Backgrounds

Although only 44, Philip had three mental scars: his father's death, a divorce, and a recent business failure. And now in midlife, his health was acting up. His dad died before retirement—would that happen to Philip, too? With poor stamina and prematurely receding graying hair, was he closing in on perpetual retirement? Before returning to work, some proactive health care was necessary. Philip determined to find answers from intelligent caring doctors, to walk often, get more sleep, and get nutrition.

On his second walk with Judi, he talked about his book: "I'm thinking of changing the title. *The Terminus* sounds too much like *The Terminator*! What do you think of *Shad Point?*"

"I like it," Judi laughed. "Like Peyton Place! Have you published any others?"

"No," Doug admitted; "This is my first try."

Lack of stamina penalized Doug while running his business. He was exhausted and his heart was beating from the stress, until a routine blood pressure test found hypertension.

"Because of my belly, I wonder if my exercise club should be resumed; but friends say walking outdoors works wonders, although it's a slow process."

"How often do you walk?" Judi asked.

"For two weeks, I've walked three times a week."

"Did you ever hike before?"

"No."

"Well then, I'd say you're doing pretty good!"

"But Judi, what do you do if the weather is lousy?"

"I walk inside Wal-Mart."

"Tell me about your business," Judi asked.

"After the factory closed, I ran a hi-tech business for five years, but the cost of technology ran up faster then profits. I finally sold it at a loss. The long hours and lousy diet almost killed me. I'd rather be a live flop than a dead success; preferably a free man than a bankrupt one; a failure rather than a fanatic. I sold the business last December and ever since, have been as happy as a clam in that marsh."

"George Santayana, who died in 1952, was a brilliant philosopher. He's called an American philosopher although he spent many years in Europe. Some of his statements speak directly to me. Although I'm in general agreement when I read his papers and appreciate the positive changes they work on others, the solitary role isn't for me. I'm too gregarious— I love to talk to others. And always have. I talk to everyone: my brother and sister, my kids, my Army buddies, my friends, and even my ex after our divorce. Here's some of Santayana's thoughts:

"Habit is stronger than reason."

"Wisdom comes by disillusionment."

"Intelligence is quickness in seeing things as they are."

"Are you a college grad, Judi?" He asked to confirm his observation.

"I graduated from Smith as an English major and then worked for two years at Harcourt as an assistant editor."

"Why only two years?"

"I became a stay-at-home mom," she explained.

"Do you do any writing?"

"Too much nervous energy! I can't sit still. That's why I walk."

Philip searched for a positive comment. "You're very intelligent and color-coordinated—even to the spaniels."

"Thanks, I was a dirty-blonde until graduation. Now, I'm using a brown rinse."

"Well, it's very attractive, Judi." Philip guessed she was around 40. As they walked, sporadic quacks came from wood frogs, loudly searching for mates like Philip.

"Did you go to college?" Judi asked.

"Yes; I met an Army vet and we got permission to commute to URI together. I majored in Liberal Arts. My job at Electric Boat was terminated after 20 years."

Judi probed again, "Do you live in this area?"

"Mystic. I live by myself. My three kids are at UConn and I help when I can. But walking is great because it's free.

"Since you're an English major, Judi; do you go to the three spring and three fall poetry readings at the Mystic Arts Center?"

"No. My husband gets home too tired on Fridays; on weeknights, I have to keep an eye on my teenage girls."

Chickadees with their spring "phe-bees" were working the brush along the trail.

Without being asked, Phillip needlessly divulged information. "I'll explain about my divorce and business. A few years ago, my wife became disgusted at my lack of success. She was an executive; I was a peon. She said I was a nuisance and didn't need me anymore. We divorced."

"My settlement money was used to start the business. It was a big chance, but I always dreamed of owning a business. I taught myself the primitive software and then taught my employees. But the revisions and new software became indecipherable to me, and I promoted a whizz kid. So we had two managers. The work and hours were strenuous. Little was left after expenses. I sold the business to my assistant, to get out from under."

Judi asked, "Were you born in 1966?"

"1965."

"You're the elder statesman in the crowd. Are your folks still alive?" Judi asked.

"I see Mom every Sunday."

"Why do you live in a "high-rent district" like Mystic?

"Well, it's an exciting tourist town. Most of my friends live there. But Groton would be cheaper."

"Tell me about your Mom and Dad."

"Well, Dad's dead—I'll tell you about him on another walk. Mom's in her late eighties: feisty as ever. She uses a walker because she's fallen so often. She tries to escape from the nursing home. It's so funny when she yells, 'Call the FBI! Call the Cops!—I'm being kidnapped!' She loves to see her grandkids. Mom always gives me hell, but I ignore her. Here's a funny story about old age: Once, my stepdad took us to a restaurant that puts extra Manhattan liquor into a small open carafe. While talking I detected Mom put the open carafe into her pocketbook. 'What are you doing Mom?' My step dad retrieved it."

The weather changed quickly, a squall developed, and they hustled back to their cars. But not soon enough—the downpour drenched them completely. They laughed it off in the parking area. Strangely enough, only one small snow storm, occurred in March.

INTERRUPTIONS IN LIFE

Chapter 4: Sculptors and Problems

On the next hike, Judi spoke about herself: "I'm fidgety and can't concentrate long enough. Walking has a calming effect. I got pregnant after a company cocktail party because I didn't trust birth control pills. We married and found this wooded retreat near the train station; my husband takes the train to the city for the week."

"I'd like to be a writer like you, but I need lots of solitude—a separate computer room away from phones, kids, and dogs."

"Smith's a great college. What was your class?"

"The class of 1989."

Judi was 41. She guarded her privacy so Philip asked fewer personal questions. Although she wouldn't divulge her name, he was happy to be walking with her. Idiosyncrasies didn't matter. He had a partner, an interesting, walking partner.

She needed a walking partner, too. Although intelligent, Philip was a blabbermouth. It was good that she used a false name. She never knew that he discovered her correct name. Walking was an interesting way to exercise. Normally, she looked forward to it. They met at the trailhead in lower Liberty Monday and Friday mornings.

If one was 15 minutes late, the other took off. After heavy ice and snow in December and January, the weather now was okay. The snow had melted by February. The sun was higher in the sky. Twice, because of rain, they walked around the inside perimeter of "Wal-Mart." Many mornings were overcast, but cleared by 9 am. Skunk cabbage grew in the damp swales and small brooks. Male wood frogs were quacking in vernal pools.

But then Phillip blurted something he regretted: "My ex always said I was stuck in my 'comfort zone' and couldn't get out of it. She said I was a creature of habit, who was happy doing simple things. But I didn't want to do exciting things; I loved the comfort of setting back and reading the paper. I was always tired from work and the never-ending 'to-do' list! I suppose my health contributed to it, also. That's the reason we broke up. This winter, with more time on my hands, I'm trying new things, healthwise and cultural. For example, I've gotten a fresh perspective on goings-on at the Arts Center and in the art world. I'm writing a book. I go to poetry readings. I've been a docent at a museum. I'm a regular at the library.

They began talking about college.

Judi asked, "Who was your most admired professor?"

"That's easy. Professor Robinson in Ancient History who boomed, "Break the mold!" to wake nodding sleepyheads. They startled awake. Years later, while trying to get to the end of the endless suburban "To-do" list, I thought of his aphorism—I was doing just the opposite, a compliant creature of an elite entertainment society."

"Oh, occasionally I deviated from the established routine. For years I helped a priest that everyone detested, that never had a chance. My friends deserted him because they didn't get their way and formed their own sect. Eventually he cracked up from years of criticism and ostracism. He died 10 years ago. Although I maintain contact with my former friends, I believed then, and still believe, they were hypocrites."

"But I couldn't apply Dr. Robinson's maxim until I sold the business. Then, with planning I really "broke the mold!" I attended as many intellectual events as I could.

Judi asked, "Was URI a planned campus? Or did it just grow?"

"A lot of good planning went into it. Although the Quad on top of the hill dates back to the Land Grant College era, the planners saw the future demand and during the Depression filled in a large hillside quarry; and after the war, moved athletics down onto the open pastures, and constructed buildings on the now-available hillside."

Without being asked, Judi continued their conversation. "Though I'm an English major, my most memorable professor was in history. Professor Zimmer published several books on women in American History. I loved the paper she wrote about female forerunners and contemporaries of Thoreau. A daughter of James Fenimore Cooper wrote a nature almanac four years before

Walden."

"Women lose so many years and brain cells in their child-rearing years. That's what I'm faced with. But pretty soon I'll be free like you, with time to gather material, peruse it, and organize it into a manuscript. The first one will be about early female ministers and critics of the Puritan church in New England, such as Ann Hutchinson, E. Fonef Winthrop, and Jemima Wilkinson."

"Smith College is the largest privately endowed college for women in the country. The initial planning was good; in 1890 Frederick Olmstead designed the grounds with botanical gardens and an arboretum. But since then, growth has overwhelmed the planning."

They were at a delightful level of frankness with each other. Using this base, Philip tried a different approach, at the end of their hike.

"Would you go with me to see a special arts exhibition, "Faces of Gaia, Mother Earth" by Ann Flower?"

"I have to be careful where I go and who I see. I'm still married, you know. Where is it being held?"

"At the Mystic Art Association."

"Do you know anything about the show? "She asked.

"Ann is an environmental artist. She scavenges the fields and woods for material to use. Then, she tries to educate the public. The newspaper showed two different fans and a large composite green cross, but friends tell me the most spectacular and controversial piece is mother earth giving birth to nature. Ann also made large imitation plant shoots, weaving upwards from pots towards the ceiling. Flower says everything is part of nature, a oneness of things."

"What time?" Judi asked

"All afternoon, free parking, free-will donations."

"I think I'll go. I'm really interested in the concept."

Philip asked, "What time is best? While the kids are in school?"

"I'll meet you at noon inside the bookstore."

The next day, while Philip registered, Judi couldn't wait and rushed to find "Mother Earth." Philip found her staring: "It's really erotic, isn't it?" Plants and birds erupted from her crotch. The plastic plant shoots in the next room looked like glossy sawbrier whips.

Ann's husband was a sculptor, also, who made exquisitely polished square metallic tubes and containers for a different concept: the unlike colors of ice. He produced tubes of imitation ice cores. Even his purposely-ragged edges, an artistic rendering of soft snow ice being plunked by three fist-sized boulders, were polished.

However, viewers were put-off by the extremely awkward pseudo-scientific titles. The couple taught at the Rhode Island School of Design.

Afterwards, Judy thanked Philip several times. "The show was great—amazingly thought-provoking. And for a small town, that building is beautiful!"

Outside, Philip remarked, "The sculptress was pretty. But she had a wine-colored nose. Do all artists drink? Is it a salve for their wounds? Does it help them delve deeper into their visions?" Doug had uncorked observations for future use.

INTERRUPTIONS IN LIFE

***

However, days later, when they hiked on Friday, Judi's attitude was skewed to the practical. She bluntly asked, "Why did you sell your business?"

"Judi, rest up a minute, please." Philip caught his breath.

Without divulging the proceeds, he retold the story: "I sold my business because technology was catching up faster than I anticipated, the software was devilishly complicated; and we had too many managers. I'm taking a long vacation and trying new things. I'm applying Dr. Robinson's 'Break the Mold!' This year, I'll get a refund on taxes. But the brutal hours of business advanced a case of hypertension. Medicine, sleep, and walking are reducing my blood pressure. In late spring, I'll take a part-time job at the Seaport, maybe 30 hours a week. I don't mind working weekends."

Philip could be blunt, too. He asked, "Why do you go to the doctor every week?"

"He's watching a pimple on my neck that he thinks will go away. It's one of the reasons I've been so nervous. The other reasons are my teenage girls and my husband. Isn't that enough justification?" She sounded loud and annoyed.

For once Philip shut up and walked.

After awhile, Judi said, "I didn't mean to bite your head off It's just overwhelming." At the trailhead, Philip kissed her cheek. She hugged him tightly. "Thanks for listening to an old lady." "Hey," he said, "I'm the senior citizen here!"

"Not when you're walking faster!" She laughed. "See you next Monday?"

"But of course, mon cher." The relationship looked rosy.

On Monday, Judi didn't show. Philip waited. "Something must have come up." He walked by himself, but it wasn't as much fun.

Friday Philip inquired, "If I might be nosy—Did you have another fight last weekend?"

"He got drunk on the club car and demanded sex right away. If there's anything that turns me off, its alcohol and shouting. He was so mad, I thought he would beat me. But he grabbed his suitcase and left. I guess the car is at the Westerly train station. He hasn't called so I don't know what's going on."

"I think he has a girlfriend, another young assistant editor, because that's his style. At least that's what my contact in the City says. He's had a series of girlfriends. I'm waiting for the kids to finish high school before I file for divorce. But if he pulls another stunt like last week, I'll file right away. I avoid wine, but I wake up five times a night— sleep isn't restful. That why I'm grateful to talk to someone from another village."

Philip made a suggestion: "From our conversations this month, Judi, it appears you need a mild tranquilizer. We're getting to the age when problems begin to happen. My idol Santayana wrote: 'Those who cannot remember the past are condemned to repeat it.' Don't let nervousness fester or it might develop into a full-blown problem! Look at the snowy egrets 'working the edge of the marsh' and the skunk cabbage growing in that swale. The buds are swelling on the maples. Salamanders are migrating to vernal pools. The loud quacking last week wasn't ducks; it was wood frogs. Ospreys have returned. Life is renewing itself. If we're lucky, soon we'll see oystercatchers. Please don't be mad about my suggestion."

"Would it surprise you if I'm already on Xanax?" asked Judi.

A moment later, she asked, "Philip, I know this sounds stupid, but what in the world is an oystercatcher?"

"Dan, my Texas friend, asked the same question. They're a conspicuous large brown/black/white shorebird that's returning to New England after federal protection. They insert their long red blade-like bills into shellfish, cutting their muscles, on pebbly shores or marsh edges. They only gather in flocks during migration or in the winter.

"Dan is my oldest friend. We grew up together in Rhode Island. We did everything from sandlot football to escapades in his skiff Now, we make Friday afternoon phone calls. He lives in South Texas. We laugh about the summer heat in Texas and politicians."

"In my backpack is a narrative poem, *Keep it on Going, Down the Line!* about my family. I'm working on it for Shad Point." He said, "Tell me what you think?"

Judi cautioned, "Are you sure? I only have time to scan it" Curious, she began and from her questions, he knew she was contemplating the story. "That's pretty good, Philip. What are you going to do with it?"

"Give copies to my kids. It's a father's duty to preserve as much family history as possible."

Chapter 5: Philip Schultz

"Since you're interested in poetry, tell me about one of the new poets," Judi said.

"Philip Schultz was born in Rochester. He began his career as an 'itinerant lecturer.' After founding a creative writing program at NYU in 1984, he started his own private writing school. It was 15 years before he published more poetry. He won the Pulitzer in 2008. Schultz's best pieces are about his past and family. Many say he's too pessimistic. Others, like me, think differently: passion is necessary, otherwise poems are fake sugar-coated greeting cards. Schultz was influenced by art, the emotional deaths of his grandmother, and father, and his dog. Here's an emotional poem, *The One Truth,* about Philip's father from *Failure,* the book that won the Pulitzer Prize:"

The One Truth

After dreaming of radiant thrones
for sixty years, praying to a god
he never loved for strength, for mercy,

INTERRUPTIONS IN LIFE

after cocking his thumbs
in the pockets of his immigrant schemes,
while he parked cars during the day
and drove a taxi all night,
after one baby was born dead
and he carved the living one's name
in windshield snow in the blizzard of 1945,
after scrubbing piss, blood,
and vomit off factory floors
from midnight to dawn,
then filling trays with peanuts,
candy, and cigarettes
in his vending machines all day,
his breath a wheezing suck
and bellowing gasp
in the fist of his chest,
after washing his face, armpits
and balls in cold back rooms,
hurrying between his hunger
for glory and his fear
of leaving nothing but debt,
after having a stroke and
falling down factory stairs,
his son screaming at him
to stop working and rest,
after being knocked down
by a blow he expected all his life,
his son begging forgiveness,
his wife crying his name,
after looking up at them
straight from hell, his soul
withering in his arms—
is this what failure is,

to end where he began,
no one but a deaf dumb God
to welcome him back,
his fists pounding at the gate—
is this the one truth,
to lie in a black pit
at the bottom of himself,
without enough breath
to say goodbye
or ask forgiveness?

In the Shad Point woods, dark brown, yellow edged "mourning cloak" butterflies fluttered past. Woodpeckers, blue jays, and goldfinches caused a racket, along with the early migrated phoebes, red-winged blackbirds, and grackles. Club Moss poked up between leaves on the forest floor. It was a lovely early spring day.

"Would you like to eat a lobster with me at the 'Water Line?' We can see if the 'parade' of powerboats and sailboats has started."

Once again she refused, "I'd love to Philip, but someone is sure to see us and rumors would start." At the mention of lobsters, she inquired, "I don't remember any pots at Shad Point; why aren't lobsters found there?"

"When strangers think of the coast," Philip replied, "they think of lobsters and rocky headlands. They're correct. This area is too marshy for lobsters. They thrive in cold, shallow, rocky water with hiding places from codfish, harbor seals, and haddock."

INTERRUPTIONS IN LIFE

Chapter 6: "Egg-Timer Riddle"

One day they took a longer, northerly path in the woods and wound up near the AMTRAK underpass. They rested on a fallen log. Philip knew Judi was aware of the benefits of exercise, but she had never heard this quote about solitude:

> "The three-way linkage between quiet alone-time, the biological functioning of the brain, and stress-related health problems is well understood, though its complexities are still being unraveled."

R

Philip began a monologue about his research on the centuries-old question: "Can you walk or jog yourself back to health? It's working for me now, but will it work in the critical years of the '60s. Will it work for everyone?"

"One theory says, depending on genes, the human body has a fixed number of heartbeats, like all electrical circuits, like batteries, like cell phones, like microwaves. The count is started when we're born. If one chooses to jog, run, do aerobics, walk fast, or work hard regularly, more heartbeats are used and we die sooner. But others claim that well-toned muscles, including the heart muscle, will last longer. Walking, instead of jogging, will keep you healthy, happy, and will delay death. I call it the 'egg-timer riddle.'

Ever hear that?" asked Philip.

"No, but it's a very interesting medical mystery," Judi replied.

Philip said, "I've concluded that moderate exercise is best."

He drank water from his backpack, and passed a quote on the subject to Judi:

> "... psychologists, shamans, physicians, and spiritual leaders long have advised that our happiness and health depend on a suitable and recurring mix of love, exercise, food, pleasure, sleep, friendship, and other basic needs. A lack of these may lead to depression."

"Gerontologists," Philip continued, "have proved

that remaining active throughout life halts the loss of muscle and skeletal tissue. The news is spreading that older people should continue all the activities they enjoyed in earlier years.

"The accepted view of the aging process has been one of stiffening, rigidity and closing down. Without proper exercise, the body contracts and we lose height, strength and flexibility. As a result, our natural free range of motion is restricted so daily activities become difficult. Even such common outer symptoms of aging—poor posture, rounded shoulders, dowager's hump, closed chest, stiffness and loss of mobility—originate when we re younger and become increasingly pronounced as the years go by. Exercise is restorative in nature, helps to recharge and revitalize the body's precious stores of energy and thus helps to prevent illness, disease and degeneration."

Philip continued, "Stephen Covey, in The 7 Habits of Highly Effective People, remarked:

'Most of us think we don't have enough time to

exercise. What a distorted paradigm! We don't have time not to. We're walking about three (or four) hours a week or a minimum of 30 minutes a day, or every other day. That hardly seems like an inordinate amount of time considering the tremendous benefits in terms of the impact on the other 162-165 hours of the week.'

"In the '70s, the Committee on Aging declared that it had not found a single physical or mental condition that could be directly attributed to the passage of time—stress and diet related conditions are experienced by young and old alike.

"Your heart is the place where your body, psyche and spirit all converge," wrote Dean Ornish, in Dr. Dean Omish's Program for Reversing Heart Disease. "We know that many of the classic symptoms of aging are caused by inactivity or the wrong activity, inadequate nutrition and accumulated stress and tension."

As they resumed walking, Philip realized he had talked too long and emphasized exercise too much. He warned Judi, "Despite this hype about exercise, please remember that sufficient rest is necessary for recuperation."

Chapter 7: Lafayette's Marsh

But Friday, Philip waited in vain for Judi.

On Monday, he asked, "What happened, Judi? You're usually here on Fridays." She looked like a shipwreck with bags under her eyes. "My love and I had a fight. He went back to the City. I think he has a girlfriend."

Philip took her by the shoulder, and gave her a hug. "You need this—you're depressed. We used to call this hug a "warm fuzzy."

She brightened and hugged him back.

"Hey, what was that for?"

"I'm returning the warm fuzzy," Judi laughed.

Pleased, Philip bragged about his unsuccessful attempt to path-find across the Marsh. Shad Point, itself, has become a private association with a one-mile road running south from River Road. After passing a field, the road is marked "Private," again. For three centuries the open fields were used for pasturing sheep and cows, and growing corn and salt hay. At present secluded houses occupy the Point. From the road, only glimpses of water are seen between tall spindly trees, growing since the decimation of the '38 and '54 hurricanes.

Lafayette's marsh is still on the west side. The salt hay from this marsh was sold to the French at Newport during the Revolution. Beforehand, Philip got directions, but mixed them up. He was supposed to take the second dirt road on the right; which had a stone ford for crossing the creek. However, he took the first. His crossing point looked wrong—too deep, so he walked north across the marsh toward the family cemetery on the trail until he was completely enveloped by the thick phragmites. The reeds were so tall he had to use the sun as a reference. His sneaker pulled off at the muddiest spot and Doug lost his balance. He caught himself in time, pulled out the sneaker, retied the laces and pushed through thousands of reeds to cross to the northern side. The distance? A tenth of a mile? He would never do it again!

Judi told him, "You don't look any worse for the adventure." "I use a black rinse." She laughed!

A few naturalists claim the reed is natural; most say it's one of the increasing number of invasives decimating the native species. Nothing eats, or lives, in phragmites.

Chapter 8: The Shed and Prohibition

A "shed" is a large, strongly built structure, often open at the sides or end. It can also be a small or crude structure built for shelter, storage, etc. A "barn" is a large farm building with doors for grain or livestock.

Was the building at Shad Island a barn, or large shed?

Judi guessed a shed was built on former "Stanchion Island" with a bridge over the marsh. Since the Stonington literature is silent about police activity during the prohibition era, one can only assume that plenty of local bootlegging was going on. Prominent families made fortunes. The fast rum-runners loaded up outside the three mile limit off Montauk and slipped into small coves along the sheltered coast. Was the shed used?

***

Philip was becoming very attached to his friend. Was he in love or was it just infatuation? He looked forward so much to their get-togethers. They talked about interesting things, not the caricatures seen on TV.

However, Judi planned to skip both hikes next week. She was going to the city.

Chapter 9: Restoration of Marriage and Nature

Judi and her husband made up; they returned from the City to tie up loose ends: the dogs were given to the pound, the lease on the house and furniture settled, the girls sent to a prep school, and the car sold at a loss.

She determined to walk once more with Philip. Looking back, he recognized the pattern: Judi had asked probing financial and personal questions. Months ago, she had dismissed the idea of him as a lover, but didn't want to discourage him altogether because he was a hard-to-find, safe, interesting walking partner.

For Philip, Judi was a pleasure to walk with, someone proud to accompany. At other times, he sensed a forthcoming brush-off and this was it!

Judi and her husband were planning an early June, Caribbean vacation to sort out their plans for the future. She wouldn't be able to walk with Philip, anymore.

"Are you moving to the City?"

"Probably—neither of us likes the country. There's room for all of us in the loft. I haven't decided whether to go back to work or to try free-lance writing, Thanks for teaching me about wood frogs, the 'egg-timer riddle,' and phragmites. Good-bye, my friend." And with a peck on the cheek, she was gone, another migrant to the big city.

***

The DEEP claims the ongoing salt marsh incursion of all-exclusive phragmites into spartina territory appears to be stabilizing in the Shad Point Marshes. A botanical and biological study by Connecticut College disclosed that the damage done by the impoundment of dikes in the late 40's was reversed by the 1982 installation of 2.1 meter culverts. Tidal flushing increased plant and shorebird activity; and slowed the spread of phragmites across these marshes. Muskrats that disappeared after the impoundments have returned to the upper Marsh. The Connecticut DEP believes the number of shad in the Liberty River has been constant for at least the past decade. Is a higher volume of water required to restore their numbers? Or is pollution still a problem? Philip believed the problem was still pollution, and also dams.

Judi and her husband moved to the city like ghost-riders, leaving no traces. Years later, Philip met his relaxed friend on the trail. She quickly said goodbye. It made him feel like a shad, swimming against the current. It's not only fish that get caught in seines.

INTERRUPTIONS IN LIFE

Chapter 10: Dad

For years, Philip remembered his talks with Judi, his colorful oystercatcher. His friend Dan wasn't sympathetic: "She wasn't so hot-Just another intellectual." But the memory of her jogged on, whenever he passed over their favorite red maple knoll, where she had asked a sensitive question:

"Philip, please tell me more about your father?"

"Would you like to hear about his last days, and the changes to mine, as well?"

"Will it bother you?"

"Yes," Philip said, "but it helps to get through the healing process. My father was more like me than my siblings. We thought alike. He was honest, loyal, religious, with a classic hairline. His loyalty did him in. My mother tried to resuscitate him with heavy meat roasts, late night dancing, and sex. Sleep would have been a better therapy."

"Decades ago in the upstairs bedroom, I scratched Dad's back, the luxury in sickness he liked best. We talked of news of the outside world that was meaningless to both of us, like the weather and the moon program. In Dad's lifetime, affection wasn't shown between men.

"I never told my father how much I loved him, and it bothers me! He never said he was proud of me and that bothers me, too. I know he was wrong-that was not the way to raise kids. Although my wife agreed to have kids; her career came first. I made up for her by giving them pride and respect."

"I should have recorded the conversations with Dad in a journal, but after the drive home I was exhausted. Most of our conversations are forgotten; generations of family history lost."

Epilogue: Tami

Philip was running out of money. At a Mexican restaurant, he met Tami, a plain chunky mother from Mystic, who had to supplement her income for her family. After securing a part-time job at the Mystic Seaport, he swallowed his pride and moved into her third floor apartment.

Summer nights when he worked at security, Tami fed the kids, read a story or two, put them to sleep, and then loved the hell out of Philip. She wasn't pretty or intelligent and disliked walking. The haphazardness of matchmaking and relationships made him wonder: "It isn't at all like buying a new car; you can't get every feature you want!"

The intervals became longer now, but Philip recalled the Brittany Spaniels and Judi's pert nose. He wondered, "Can intelligence and beauty ever be a substitute for love?" During those moments, Philip often thought of Judi. Was she a colorful oystercatcher that pried open intellectual shells? Or was his friend Dan right that "Judi was a "ball-buster!"

Philip subscribed to *Time*; continued to write, and attended poetry sessions; all in the optimistic dream of resuming his intellectual years.

At first it was tentative, but gradually the tender relaxation offered by love, writing, and walking, made him appreciate his plain girlfriend. He could tell by her actions and laughter that she loved him, so much so that her love amazed him. She was a sensitive and caring human being. The experience was new to him and he was grateful.

Similar to the DEEP's reversal in the Shad Point marshes, a change in habits and circumstances had accidentally brought him the love and contentment that he had been seeking all his life.

A woman's love and respect is the ultimate! Intellectualism with its dogfights be damned.

Sources:

Failure, by P. Schultz

Groton Public and Westerly Libraries

Denison Pequotsepos Nature Center

The 7-Habits of Successful People, S. Covey

Wikipedia

DEEP

The Davis-Stanton Homestead, John Davis
   (now deceased)

Various, Santayana

Tom Douglas

Mystic Arts Center and Ann Flower

Audubon Field Guides

Stillness, R. Mahler

Dr. Dean Ornish's Program for Reversing Heart Disease

Keep it on Going, Down the Line, by B.D. Boylan

INTERRUPTIONS IN LIFE

Kokoncke:
Dodkin's Lost Sheep

A Novella

Bernard D. Boylan

2016, 2017

Table of Contents.......*Kokoncke: Dodkin's Lost Sheep*

Preface

Prologue

Chapter 1: The Marsh

Chapter 2: Mary Ann's Open Wounds

Chapter 3: Jack's Partial Recovery

Chapter 4: Mary Ann and the Institution of Marriage

Chapter 5: Walks: Hikes by Joe and Jack

Chapter 6: The Docility of Sheep

Chapter 7: Kokoncke and Bill's "Golden Flower"

Chapter 8: The Lost Sheep in Matthew 18:10-14

Epilogue: Dodkin's Lost Sheep

Sources

Preface:

First of all, let's emphasize that this is fiction. Although the area's historical background was introduced to me by books and walks with my friend Joe, the characters and plot are figments of my imagination.

Kokoncke is a novella, longer than a short story but the appropriate length to tell a tale that won't unduly jeopardize my endurance. The remainder of my career will be occupied with stories of this size.

A significant part of any author's compensation is knowledge gained by research. Before *Kokoncke,* I didn't know anything about sheep, but see Chapter 6 for information gained.

Mary Ann in Chapter 2 began as a genuine encounter on the back stairs of the library and was expanded into multiple chapters story. My Yankee friend, Joe, had a different name. He was so similar, reliable, patriotic, and cheerful that his real name should have been recorded and honored. But because of the (unexpressed) threat of libel, I was forced to do otherwise.

Though my kids have moved to other states, this was a wonderful area to raise them. For more on child-raising, see my book "A New England Quatrain."

I hope you enjoy reading this as much as I did composing it.

Bernie, 2017

Prologue: Kokoncke

One late spring morning, Jack and his friend Joe amused themselves in a marina by searching for boat transoms from the most distant location. They found one from Barbados, before leaving the marina on the northwestern shore of Ali's Island. The two veterans resumed their walk, picking up their pace as they headed for the nearby roads of an upscale development, one that actually improved the view of the village of Misty View. Since the growth of trees all over town, views of the water and almost everything has gradually disappeared. According to the accounts of early colonists, the Native Americans had periodically burned these hillsides to cultivate huckleberries, a staple of their diet. Now, residents of streets with proud marine images could no longer see the waters of Long Island Sound or even their own village.

But on their shoreline walks, every week Jack and Joe witnessed the Sound, river, harbor, and marshes. One of those marshes was named Kokoncke, a Native American word that defies translation.

Long before Joyce Kilmer's poem "Trees," worship of trees and groves existed and Jack, himself, loved their beauty and hated to see large trees cut down, whatever the reason. Others, such as banks, insurance agencies, utilities, and towns have urged removal. Perhaps the cost of heating and home repair has upset the balance.

Chapter 1: The Marsh

As Joe and Jack approached the causeway to the mainland, a boat from the livery passed underneath and sped by them, heading for the sound. Jack asked, "Is the water deep?"

Joe reminded him, "the water is very shallow, perhaps three feet deep at high tide."

On the mainland side of the causeway, they said hello to a clammer in waders and khakis, who was loading gear into a pickup that was parked next to a fence and a marsh.

"How was the clamming," Jack asked.

"Real good, but the water was so cold, I didn't stay long. We're expecting guests and I'm treating them to 'clams casino'" (a popular appetizer at shore restaurants).

Behind him was the widely irregular shape of Kokoncke marsh where sheep were grazing on short marsh grass.

Joe suggested, "Let's walk up this hillside to Bill

Dodkins's house and say hello." While ascending the empty slope, Jack turned frequently to admire the view—it improved every time he turned. He urged, "Let's stop a minute." At the top of the hill, the sheep looked like tiny cotton balls and the panorama of the lower river and sound was spectacular: the myriad blue/green configurations of a glacially drowned coastline, cradled white hulls and dense aluminum "forests" at busy marinas, expensive mansions with water vistas, and aerial views of islands. But except for the speedboat, no boating activity.

"Where's the boats, Joe?"

"The owners are waiting for Memorial Day, the traditional start of the boating season. In the meantime they'll have plenty of jobs around their boats to get ready for the season. After uncovering the blue canvas or the white shrink-wrap, the engines and water systems will have to be recommissioned, some painting done, and possible corrosion removed from fixtures."

"What a view, Joe! It's fabulous. How do you know Bill?"

"I've known him all my life. He's older but our families attended services and many church suppers together. A few years ago I was his last financial planner. Every once in a while I pop in to say hello. He's 95 years old and wants to stay here with his cherished view and his sheep until he dies. He's been offered millions for the property but refuses every offer. He's a real Yankee"

Though Jack loved this little town, he would never be a native. The locals tolerated his work but treated him differently. He was surprised when Joe accepted his offer to walk for an hour three mornings a week. Apparently, no one else was available. Many of Joe's friends spent mornings at the local coffee and donut shop, but he battled diabetes by diet and walking. Jack knew better than to complain about discrimination; he was glad to have a partner to walk with.

Decades ago, while raising his family, Jack had been to Bill's restaurant many times; so when Joe repeated area history, "Bill's river front restaurant was torn down for an automobile dealership," Jack just nodded.

The two men knocked on the door, but a caregiver said Bill was napping. They left a message and took a narrow road to the well-traveled winding island road, walking single-file for safety, and returned to their cars at the boat livery.

"I wanted," Joe said, "to ask Bill about his sheep. He doesn't need the money. I don't know why he keeps them? But I'll ask some other time." Time is often shorter than we think.

Chapter 2: Mary Ann's Open Wounds

Although spring 2005 was late, the rapid rise in temperatures accompanied by strong sunlight made seasonal indicators pop up everywhere: skunk cabbage, red maples, crocuses, brilliant yellow of male goldfinches, and the return of ospreys, snowy egrets, and clammers!

The librarians gladly helped Jack for so much research, that today he felt like a Pulitzer winner. At noon, as Jack left the Library on its sunken sidewalk, sheltered by a row of unusual cultivated hydrangea, he chatted with a retired woman who was sitting on the steps to the parking lot while reading the paper. "It's so warm, quiet, and peaceful here," she confided with a big smile. Most people, especially women, hardly ever sit on concrete. Are they afraid of cold fannies? Despite that possibility she had resourcefully made use of this quiet nook and was glad to talk.

"This morning, we walked along the northern side of Ali's Island and saw the fabulous panorama from the hill above Kokoncke marsh. We also saw the truest sign of spring: a clammer." They laughed.

She was his age, mature, intelligent, and interesting. Though he didn't know her name, they talked for about 15 minutes. He could see that she was pleasant and gracious, had a big smile, and perhaps was lonely. He decided to find out because he, himself, was terribly lonely. Jack could only concentrate for 4 hours of writing and searched for alternate places to write and occupy his time besides the telephone. The library had two or three spots and McDonald's one for mid-afternoon. He had pestered friends too often.

She hadn't excused herself, wasn't in a hurry and continued talking. If she was married she would have ducked away. Possibly she could be a good friend.

"Jack, I know who you are," she said," though you don't remember me, I was one of your customers. I'm Mary Ann. My friends told me you could reduce the size of a legal document and on the third attempt you did it. Then you refused to charge me for the extra scrap and time. It was a charitable gesture. I was impressed."

"You're an interesting woman—I'd like to talk more, but my stomach is rumbling. Would you like to walk to the pizza place to continue our conversation?"

Mary Ann knew a little about Jack—he was a gentleman. She wanted to learn more and her intuition told her to take a chance. She stood up, brushed off, and walked with him to the restaurant. She ordered two plain slices and Jack four with pepperoni. While waiting to be served, they decided to talk about an innocuous topic, their hometowns. Other topics could follow.

"I came," Jack said, "from an aging egalitarian neighborhood near Providence, RI. My small bedroom was stifling. Why didn't I decorate it for better use for me and my friends? Now I decorate with colorful prints by famous artists. Both parents died penniless so after paying the remainder of their funeral expenses, I was left nearly broke." It was usually a mistake to say this, but he let his dates know his constraints and their attitude forewarned him about them.

When Mary Ann's turn came, she switched to an awful topic, one that obviously plagued her—a recent divorce. Jack knew from experience: The closer the event-the worse the hurt.

"After raising two kids, my husband and I moved to a two-story Misty View condo that had more problems than the sellers or agents revealed. The stairs were physically taxing and required trip planning to avoid burnout. If it rained, the neighbor wouldn't walk his dogs—he let them outside without a leash, against the regulations. The big dogs frightened me and other elderly residents. Parking was restricted and a large assessment was due for roofing."

She should have postponed the rest of her story. But anger made her continue the "aggrieved partner routine," to get the bitching out of her system. "My husband began staying out late too many nights. A friend told me where ills car was parked and I surprised him at his girlfriend's house. The divorce drained me emotionally. Because the kids were gone and I had a job, I settled for half of our net worth; otherwise it would have gone on for years and I simply had to get away from the torture. With the proceeds, I financed a small home near the library. The only time that my former husband contacted me and the kids was at Christmas." She had monopolized their conversation and realized her mistake, "I'll tell you the rest some other time."

Jack was a good listener—he had been through a divorce, too. But he would rather talk about anything other than his ex. He didn't want to prolong horrible memories any more. This month had been a positive one and he preferred it to continue: a self-published book, a poetry reading, symphony concert, a visit from England by his son, one from a daughter, and calls from friends.

On the other hand, Mary Ann should understand that a man can be hurt, too. Though it happened thirty years ago, his divorce hurt as badly as ever. His former wife took away the only thing that ever mattered to him—his family. Do you ever get over being rejected? The casting-off never vanished from his mind, yet experience warned him to explain only small parts of his allegations.

INTERRUPTIONS IN LIFE

Chapter 3: Jack's Partial Recovery

Every so often on their walks, Joe would tip Jack's equilibrium by inquiring about an aspect of his marriage. At first Jack gave brief answers. He was lonely and didn't comprehend how deeply his former wife's rotten treatment had affected him. But after she obtained two annulments, church and civil, he finally realized he had been shafted, especially after his reputation had tanked and the wisecracks of adults had multiplied. Jack hated to be the brunt of jokes. He took so many cheap shots that he became depressed and unusually somnolent.

His last job had been terribly boring. For years, the planners were crowded in rooms of an older building. Investor pressure led to mergers and layoffs in the boom and bust period of American industry. Though the firm had an iron-tight patent, no one needed or purchased their machines in a recession. The financial shenanigans and mergers caused by Wall Street intervention created too much debt on the corporation balance sheet.

A decade later, young managers brought enlightened changes to the manufacturing layout and built an office building across the street. Jack's new ecru cubicle was the last in a row. By monitoring, his boss noticed that Jack had the highest number of keystrokes. After finishing his jobs, he scrambled on new ones. His friend Pat and he were the last to be laid off. The job fair was useless in the recession at the end of the Cold War; only key machinists were hired.

Using his pension, Mike started a graphics business that went bankrupt in another recession. There's no way of knowing what might have happened if friends hadn't intervened. He hated to quit but took early retirement; and the next ten years were the best of his life. One by one, he resumed activities postponed since marriage: hiking, reading, a writer's group, the symphony and library lectures. He taught himself how to dance. Jack joined every area historical society until he saw that his presence was meaningless, irritating to some, and he quietly dropped out.

After Jack wrote a large number of books, his friends, children, and a doctor flattered him but urged more sleep. The initial stories were original and spontaneous, with varied plots. But then, for years he languished writing far too many articles and anthologies about artists, useless to anyone else. No one needed his opinions on artists. It took years for him to reverse and get back on track, but he finally broke out of this mental jam by getting more sleep and exercise. He found the motivation to write again, but older now, with less energy, he downsized his work habits by revising older works, lengthening short stories, and reading good fiction to keep his mind active. He wrote fewer hours.

***

Before retirement, Jack thought of searching for his friend. Pat, one of the women in the office, who seemed genuinely interested, but the divorce rankled him so badly that he didn't pursue her. He was an emotional washout, a man without a mission, who skimped on food to buy gas and tickets. Finally, he dated two completely opposite women: a buxom one who talked way too fast and a trim one who mumbled one word at a time. He stopped dating for years and moved into senior housing.

His initial "holiday" treatment by residents was followed by six months of hell. It was his only bad year. Jack moved, joined an exercise group and two years later, met Mary Ann at the Library.

By now, he had enough sense to avoid flashy broads. The distaste was mutual. They looked for money and security in a man and while he searched for character. He needed a woman who had aged naturally; someone to have intelligent conversations with; and a grownup that would understand his limited finances.

Mary Ann was a distinct possibility. After a few dates, he'd be able to figure out if she was right for him. Because of his baldness, he adored thick glossy hair on a woman, especially if they ran their fingers through it, he correctly concluded that Mary Ann's gray hair was a sign of maturity. She was a grownup, not a teenager vying for attention. When he asked if she would like to attend the next symphony, she was happy to be asked— she would never go alone.

Although his back acted up, he poked around her

yard, raking and bagging a few pockets of leaves, and then, like the Army, "policing" paper, plastic bags, styrofoam, and beer cans from her front yard. Mary Ann saw him picking up outside and didn't interrupt before calling him inside for a New England beans and hotdog supper—one of his favorites. She thanked him profusely. He took a chance by confiding in Mary Ann, and she did too, but it seemed they were on the same wavelength—so far, so good! It made him feel like hollering, "I am what I am!" Or did "Popeye" say that?

INTERRUPTIONS IN LIFE

> "Marriage, to women as to men, must be a luxury, not a necessity; an incident of life, not all of it. "   - Susan B. Anthony, 1875

Chapter 4: Mary Ann and the Institution of Marriage

On their first dates, Mary Ann anticipated unwelcome moves by Jack and wondered what her response would be. But he never touched her. When her girlfriends jealously and obstinately inquired, she was embarrassed. She alibied that he was shy, but as the father of kids, that wasn't true. And a sample of his writing was plain vanilla, one hundred years behind the times—to an earlier gentler era. He was strange and different than other beer-drinking, football fanatics. Maybe, he wasn't conventional, but he was his own man, an eye-opening, kindly eccentric. His opinions and actions were original. She loved his teasing "Hey, old-timer," or "Love of my life."

Bitterness definitely affected his manhood. Slowly, parts of Jack's experience, attitudes, and personality leaked out. He was loyal and decorated graves. His education was first rate although he worshipped Thoreau, that old nemesis of consumerism. It was one of the reasons he walked with Joe—they talked about simple living and how to get more "bang for the buck." So he was economical. His savings produced books, but he got upset when so few read his work. But stubbornly, year after year, he pushed ahead, no matter the subject.

Small emotional incidents brought tears to his eyes. From what Mary Ann gathered, he stayed through the second half of his marriage, a period of mutual destruction that had almost destroyed him. He wouldn't say any more. Villagers treated him like a reject from society. It was years before his self-esteem was restored; ordinary family life never. However, in senior housing he was happy, "snug as a bug in a rug." Why disturb it.

Mary Ann was skeptical and her children were neutral. She never asked him to move in. The reasons weren't financial but obvious—she would have to give up her new hard won freedom. So the two lost sheep flocked together, for restaurants and entertainment, but wary of too much togetherness.

Chapter 5: Walks: Hikes by Joe and Jack

Almost like twins, Joe and Jack were born a month apart, wore glasses, were stationed on opposite sides of the same West German city, loved symphonic music, lived in adjoining towns, wore ball caps, and took early retirement in the same year. They thought and looked so much alike that strangers thought they were brothers. Joe took his career as a financial planner seriously and he and his wife had built a new home. He showed all the new features to Jack.

When his walking partner asked, Joe explained his struggle to overcome diabetes: "I gave up smoking, follow an extremely careful diet of unsaturated sugar and salads, walk for an hour every day, and get plenty of sleep unless the UConn women are on." At this, he laughed.

When Jack joined his walks, both men felt a renewed commitment to health and life. They looked forward to the hikes so much that neither was ever late at their rendezvous. They walked and talked along the entire lower coast of Misty View, on trails in the woods and along every spoke of Ali's Island, and often crossed another causeway to a retreat center. All the while, they discussed the news, local events, overseas travel, Army incidents, family history, and in a distinct level of trust, even differences in religion.

They drooled over many marine views. Jack's favorite spot was the magnificent headland of Ali's Point with 270 degree views of Fishers Island Sound. Though the price of the lot was fantastic, they knew it was worth every penny and since then, a huge mansion has been built on its ledge. That property was the envy of residents on the far side of the harbor, who watched the stages of its construction with awe. Joe's favorite spot was the first road curve near home, where wind direction could be discerned from sloops at moorings. Another favorite was the view of Rhode Island from the retreat center. Joe often spoke of our affinity to water.

***

After struggling with his illness for years, one morning Joe bragged to Jack, "I've licked my diabetes: my sugar levels have been dropping on every test and yesterday's reading was the lowest since retirement."

Without telling Jack, he was so excited that he bought a used convertible. The cause was unknown, but a defective front tire may have blown on I-95 and the car flipped off the highway. Jack visited but Joe died within a week. His death was a tsunami to Jack's carefully terraced life—they had matched up so well.

Jack half-heartedly resumed his search for a walking partner, but wasn't successful. He was a lost soul with infrequent solitary walks. Although he continually said "good morning" to everyone, on the inside he didn't feel "good"; the whole pattern of his life had changed.

He sized up the men in the exercise class at the senior center—all were too old, feeble, or housebound. Years passed without the benefits of fresh air. At Mary Ann's urging he walked around the inside corridors of the Senior Center. It was covered, dry, and heated and air- conditioned. He met many who knew his name. Usually after walking and exercises, Jack had lunch with Mary Ann.

Suddenly, a quiet middle-aged man in physical

therapy joined their table. Jack was really slow to realize his good fortune and ask, but finally joined his new friend for mid-day walks on trails and areas that were new to him. The renewed exploration was fun and inspiring.

But winter holidays, storms, and vacations came and Jack didn't exercise and got way out of shape for long hikes.

Perhaps, if inside walking was extended in length and frequency, outside hiking could be resumed in the Spring?

Chapter 6: The Docility of Sheep

Grazing by sheep, goats, and cattle is the traditional way of managing lowland grass and marsh habitats, because the animals control sprouting scrub and trees. Before engaging a herd, consider these factors: the availability of sheep or cattle; resources to care for them; water supply; and the absence of dogs or dog walkers.

Sheep are ruminant mammals that number over one billion, mainly in Australia, New Zealand, South America, and Great Britain. Adult females are ewes, males are rams, and younger sheep are lambs. Domesticated early in civilizations, sheep are raised for wool, meat, and milk. The wool color among breeds is varied, but mostly white like the dominant breed, "Marino sheep".

Sheep have a range of heights, weights, and growth rates. The weight of ewes is between 99-220 pounds and 99-353 pounds for rams. As ruminants, the front teeth in the lower jaw bite against a hard pad in the upper jaw and the rear teeth grind the food. Their health declines after four years as they gradually lose teeth and so the average life expectancy is about eleven years. They have good hearing, terrific peripheral vision, a good sense of smell and taste but poor depth perception.

Taste enables them to select sweet and sour plants, not bitter ones. They are herbivorous mammals that prefer to graze on grass, leaving the taller plants to goats and cattle. Their digestive system consists of four parts and like cows, food is regurgitated as a cud. Sheep can overgraze so shepherds rotate the flocks between fields. When feeding, they periodically raise their heads to check on whether the flock has moved.

They are flock animals and gregarious, which is why they were one of the first animals to be domesticated. For flocking, farmers use a leader, or trained dogs, or buckets of feed, to move herds. Though considered dumb, their IQs are equal to cattle. Their sounds range from bleats, grunts, rumbles, and snorts They recognize most colors and human faces. But they are extremely timid.

Since they are subject to panic, poisons, diseases,

and injuries, often fatally, they require more care than the peaceful images of grazing indicate. Some of their diseases are transmitted to humans. Low-stress handling is essential because excited sheep can die from panic.

INTERRUPTIONS IN LIFE

Chapter 7: Kokoncke: and Bill's "Golden Flower"

Joe never had another opportunity to inquire about Bill's sheep on the Kokoncke marsh. And the herd vanished when Bill, himself died. The reason was almost forgotten until a relative returned Jack's call.

The saga originated back in the seventies in the last year of the restaurant. Bill wanted to sell and retire, but wished to do it properly. One day a waitress suddenly quit and the very next person to see him was Mai, a short Vietnamese refugee who spoke English. She had been a waitress elsewhere, said she would be eternally grateful, and begged to be hired. Faced with the summer rush, he hired her on the spot. Every day she worked overtime and followed orders—no matter what, she did it. Bill was grateful for her help and called Mai, "Golden Flower."

When he announced the sale and demolition, Mai didn't cry like other employees but asked, "You need a housekeeper; hire me." Well, it was true: his wife was dead, he would be home all day, was in his late seventies, no longer agile, the house was multi-story, he couldn't cook. His daughters lived elsewhere, and he didn't get along with his son. Since Mai was so reliable, Bill hired her and fixed up an apartment in another building. They got along great.

Once, he caught the flu and lay in bed shivering. Mai warmed his body by crawling in bed alongside him, a young woman helping an old man. Bill survived. He remembered the Biblical passage about old King David in I Kings: 1, 1-4…

> [1] King David was old and advanced in years; and although they covered him with clothes, he could not get warm. [2] So his servants said to him, "Let a young virgin be sought for my lord the king, and let her wait on the king, and be his attendant; let her lie in your bosom, so that my lord the king be warm." [3] So they searched for a beautiful girl throughout all the territory of Israel, and found Abishag the Shunammite, and brought her to the king. [4] The girl was very beautiful. She became the king's attendant and served him, but the king did not know her sexually.

Mai's meals provided the nutrition that seniors need; often a Vietnamese recipe. She washed his clothes and each morning, laid them on his bed. At Christmas she presented him with a book, often an area history. Mai was a dedicated woman.

Though he would buy her anything, Flower rarely asked. However, about two years later, she asked, "Who owns the marsh and fence? Can I use my money and buy several ewes from a farmer?" Bill was reluctant to be tied down, but finally gave in. They converted another building to a stable. Mai was so happy leading and caring for her flock morning and night. There are multiple ways of leading sheep: by a leader, a sheep herding dog, or by carrying a bucket of feed.

The sheep got to know Flower and Bill, and followed either one. The fence kept dogs out. Once in a while, a hawk would grab a newborn, but the flock grew. Bill hired the farmer to teach her shearing and butchering. She learned fast. Often at supper, he laughed, "Lamb, again?"

Mai was so happy that she told everyone, "I've

finally found a peaceful home, away from the horrors of war." Her experiences were so frightful that she wouldn't talk about them. When a Vietnamese man visited and asked her to leave, Flower refused, "too much subservience," and continued to help Bill. Fifteen happy years went by.

***

Mai didn't believe in gloves and contacted a fatal sheep disease through the skin which

local doctors didn't know how to treat. On her deathbed, Flower begged Bill, "Will you watch my sheep?" He agreed through his tears. He paid all the funeral expenses and faithfully kept his promise. Every time he led the sheep, he thought of "Golden Flower's" loyalty.

By now, however, Bill, was quite old and soon became incapacitated. It became impossible for him to maintain the flock and he sold it to the same farmer.

Chapter 8: The Lost Sheep in Matthew 18:10-14

"Take care that you do not despise one of these little ones; for, I tell you, in heaven their angels continually see the face of my Father in heaven. What do you think? If a shepherd has a hundred sheep, and one of them has gone astray, does he not leave the ninety-nine on the mountains and go in search of the one that went astray? And if he finds it, truly I tell you, he rejoices over it more than over the other ninety-nine that never went astray. So it is not the will of your Father in Heaven that one of these little ones should be lost."

INTERRUPTIONS IN LIFE

Epilogue: Dodkin's Lost Sheep

Bill lived for a few more years and never forgot his lost sheep. He became a patron of refugees; too old to sponsor, but willing to provide financial support.

Although the origin of refugees shifted elsewhere than Vietnam, Bill remembered how happy the asylum seekers were in America. They were grateful, hard workers who weren't afraid to get their hands dirty. Did this flow, generation after generation seeking the American dream, revitalize America? Bill thought it did. After preserving the hill and Kokoncke in his will, he provided financial incentives for refugees.

Jack and Mary Ann were seen all over the Misty View area, from the symphony to breakfast restaurants. Often they walked to an outside table at a nearby deli. Jack remained friendly but determined not to get entangled, again.

When others inquired, Mary Ann was embarrassed, but with his eccentricity and her concern for safety, it was best that they were just friends. As much as she loved his nicknames and understood his reluctance, her dream of remarriage was lost. However, the comradeship of meals together, and the golden glow of friendship persisted.

Bill had a flat stone placed upon Mai's grave, next to the family's headstone. Along with her birthplace, the inscription read, "Golden Flower, a Gracious Lover of America," and every year he placed a flower until he was unable.

In his last years, he told everyone, "I'd rather be a shepherd than a wolf." Bill knew he had done more good than harm in his life—he was going to be okay.

Jack lost all contact with Joe's wife. Did she blame him for the tragedy?

Sources:

Wikipedia

The Shoreline of Southeastern Connecticut,
  by B.D. Boylan

The RSV of the *Holy Bible*

Major John Mason's Great Island, J. Allyn

INTERRUPTIONS IN LIFE

Made in the USA
Columbia, SC
29 June 2018